SHAKESPEARE ILLUSTRAT

William Shak

MACBETH

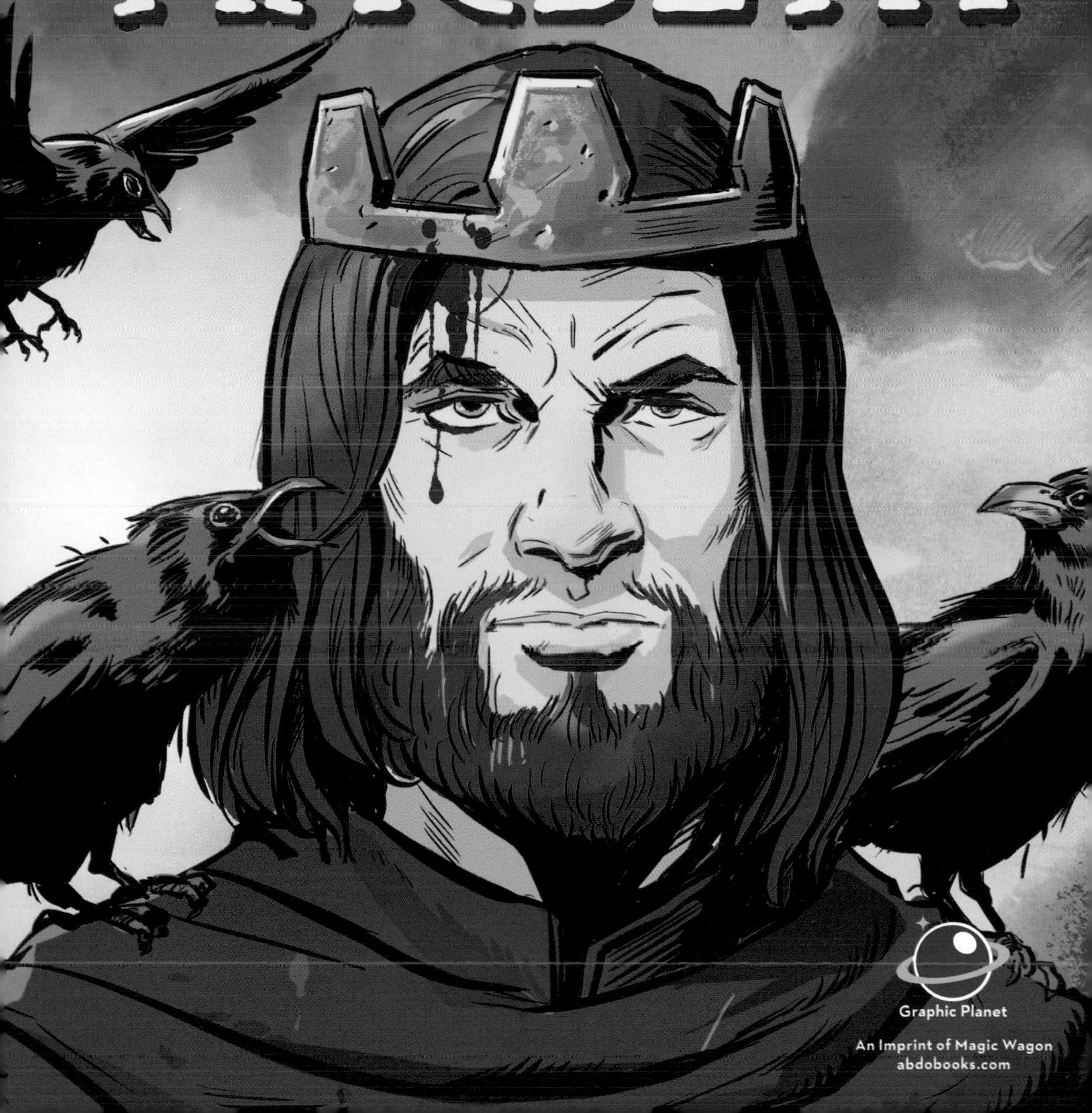

Graphic Planet

An Imprint of Magic Wagon
abdobooks.com

Published by Magic Wagon, a division of ABDO, PO Box 398166, Minneapolis, Minnesota 55439. Copyright ©
2023 by Abdo Consulting Group, Inc. International copyrights reserved in all countries. No part of this book may be
reproduced in any form without written permission from the publisher. Graphic Planet™ is a trademark and logo of
Magic Wagon.

Printed in the United States of America, North Mankato, Minnesota.
052022
092022

Adapted by Joeming Dunn
Cover art by Dave Shephard
Interior art by David Hutchison
Edited by Tamara L. Britton
Interior layout and design by Candice Keimig and Colleen McLaren

Library of Congress Control Number: 2021952008

Publisher's Cataloging-in-Publication Data

Names: Shakespeare, William; Dunn, Joeming, authors. | Hutchison, David, illustrator.
Title: William Shakespeare's Macbeth / by William Shakespeare, Adapted by Joeming Dunn; illustrated
    by David Hutchison.
Description: Minneapolis, Minnesota: Magic Wagon, 2023. | Series: Shakespeare illustrated classics
Summary: When three witches foretell that Scottish general Macbeth will be king, he and his wife decide
    to fulfill the prophecy by murdering the present king in his sleep.
Identifiers: ISBN 9781098233297 (lib. bdg.) | ISBN 9781644948439 (pbk.) | ISBN 9781098234133
    (ebook) | ISBN 9781098234553 (Read-to-Me ebook)
Subjects: LCSH: Macbeth (Shakespeare, William)--Juvenile fiction. | Macbeth, King of Scotland, active
    11th century--Juvenile fiction. | Tragedy--Juvenile fiction. | Regicides--Juvenile fiction. | Scotland--
    Juvenile fiction. | Literature--Juvenile fiction.
Classification: DDC 741.5--dc23

Table of Contents

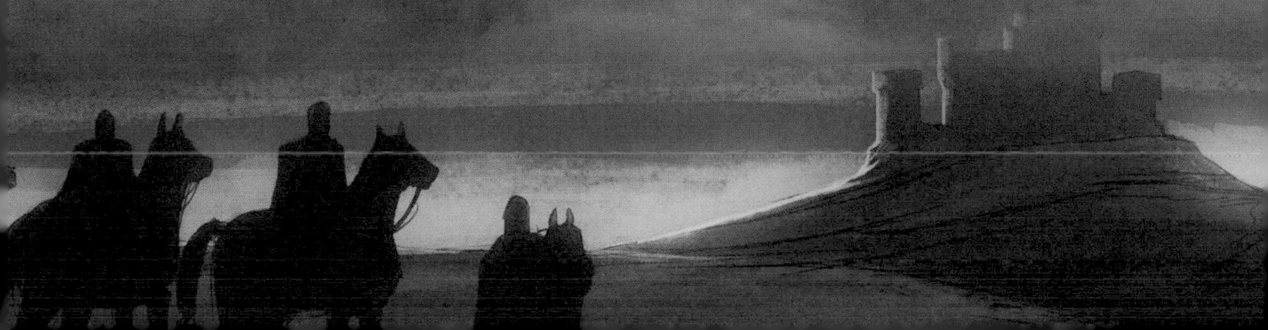

Cast of Characters

DUNCAN
King of Scotland

DONALBAIN
Son of Duncan

MALCOLM
Son of Duncan

MACBETH
*General of
Scottish army*

BANQUO
*General of
Scottish army*

MACDUFF
Scottish noble

LENNOX
Scottish noble

LORD ROSSE
Scottish noble

MENTETH
Scottish noble

ANGUS
Scottish noble

CAITHNESS
Scottish noble

LADY MACBETH
Wife of Macbeth

**THREE
ASSASSINS**

THREE WITCHES
Foretellers of Fate

FLEANCE
Banquo's son

Synopsis

Scottish generals Macbeth and Banquo defeated invading armies from Ireland and Norway. They encounter three witches while crossing a moor. The witches prophesy that Macbeth will be Thane of Cawdor and later king of Scotland. They say Banquo's descendants will include a line of Scottish kings, but he will not be king himself.

Macbeth and Banquo are skeptical of the witches' claims. But King Duncan sends men to congratulate them on their victories and also tell Macbeth that he has been named Thane of Cawdor. Macbeth thinks that perhaps the witches were right.

Lady Macbeth wants her husband to be king. She and Macbeth plan to kill King Duncan when he visits for dinner that night. That night after dinner, while King Duncan is sleeping, Macbeth kills him. In fear for their lives, the king's sons Malcolm and Donalbain leave Scotland.

Macbeth, remembering the witches' claim that Banquo's heirs would be kings, hires assassins to kill him and his son Fleance. Banquo is killed, but Fleance escapes. That night, Banquo's ghost appears to Macbeth during a feast at Dunsinane Castle. Afraid, Macbeth rages, causing the assembled nobility to doubt his leadership.

Macbeth visits the witches. They say to beware the nobleman Macduff. They tell him he can't be harmed by any man born of a woman, and that he will be safe until Birnam Wood comes to Dunsinane Castle. Macbeth is relieved. All men are born of women, and woods don't move. To be safe, when Macduff goes to visit Malcolm, Macbeth orders his family killed.

Macduff is overcome with grief when he hears about his family. He and Malcom lead an army to Dunsinane Castle to seek revenge. Preparing for the fight, Macbeth learns that Lady Macbeth has killed herself. But he believes the witches' prophecies assure his safety. Later he learns the approaching forces' shields are made of trees from Birnam Wood.

The battle ensues and Malcolm and Macduff's army soon overtake Macbeth's. When Macduff confronts Macbeth, he reveals that he was not born of a woman but delivered by cesarean section. Macduff kills Macbeth and Malcolm becomes Scotland's king.

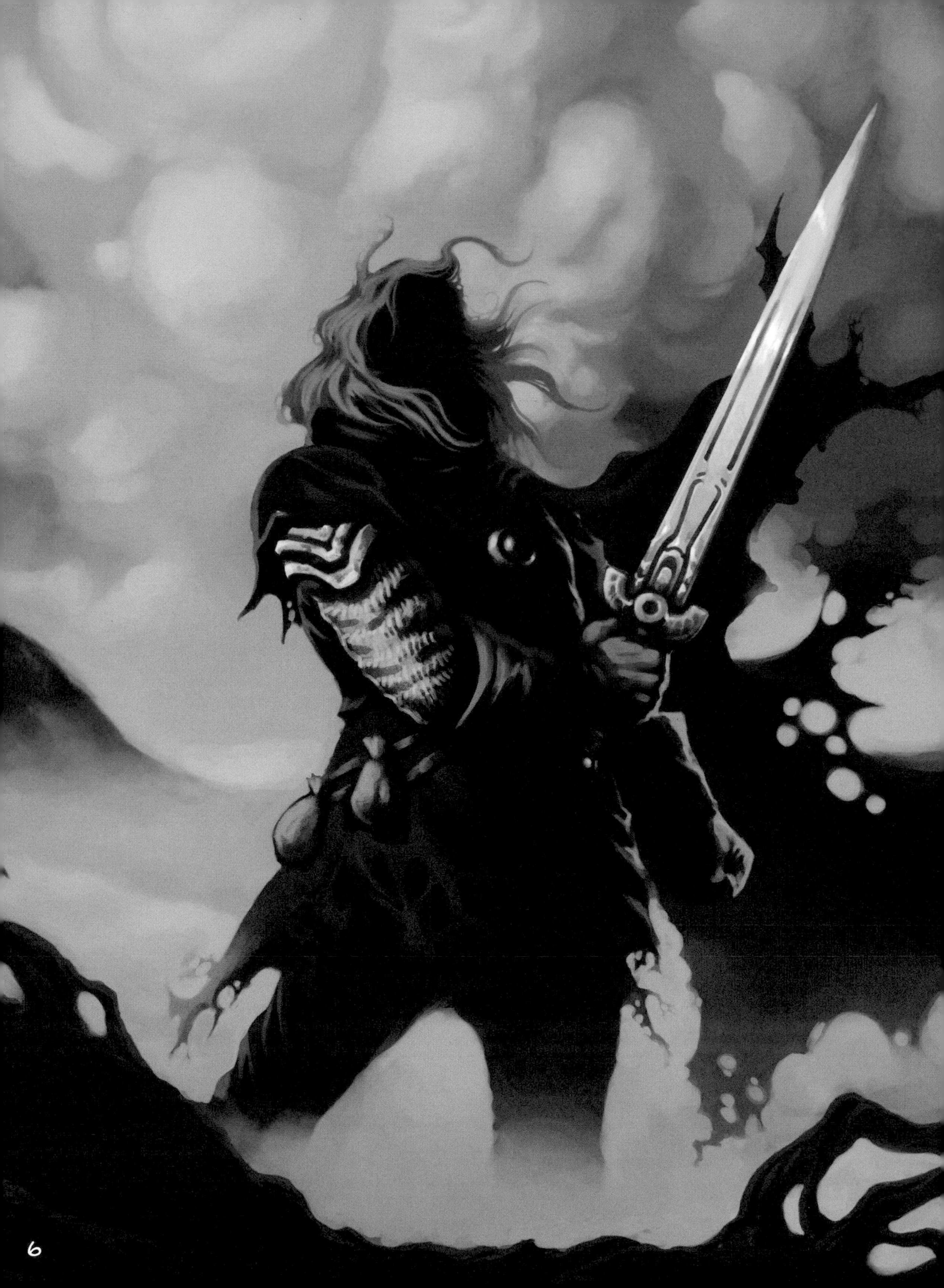

ACT I

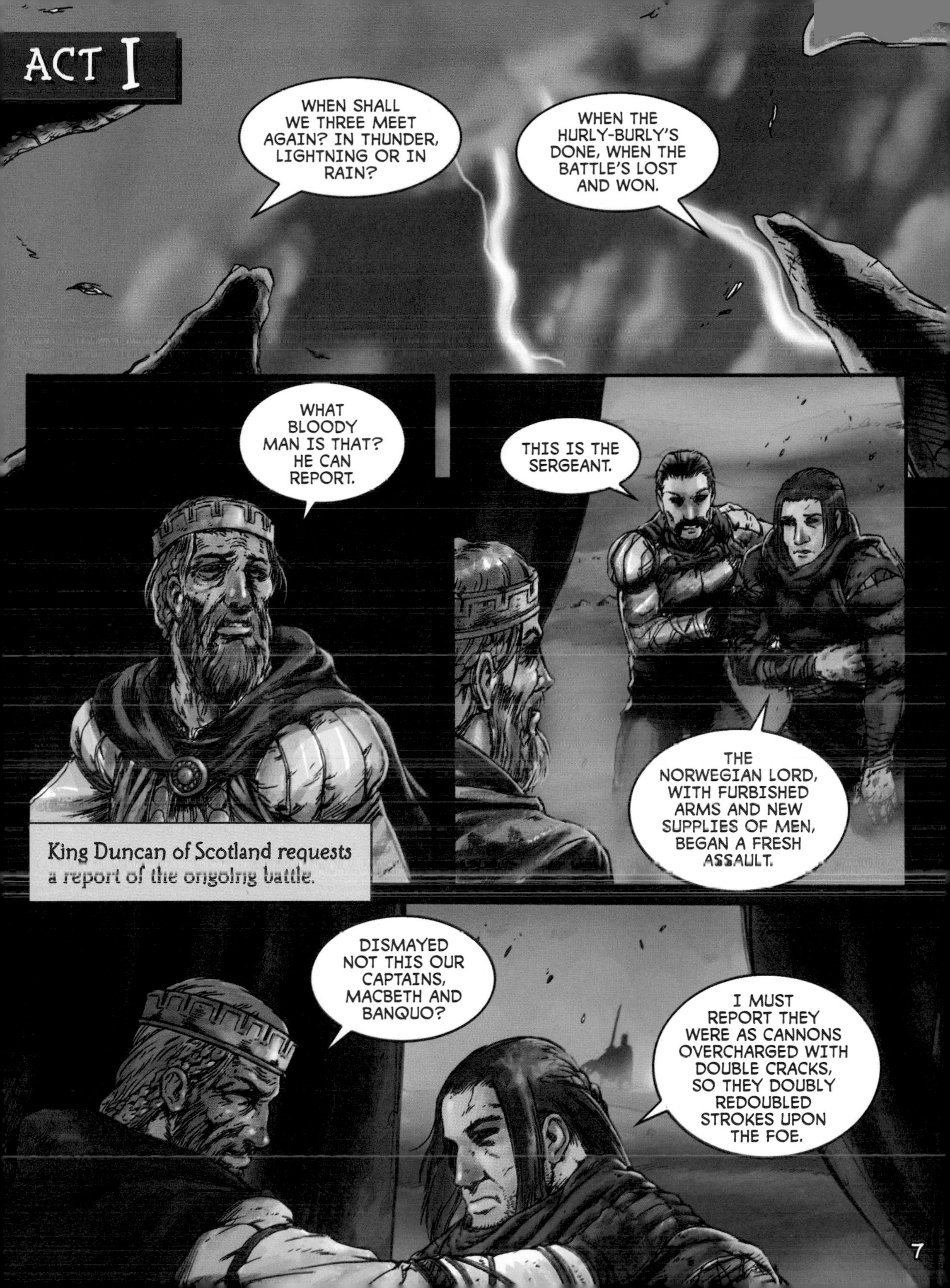
WHEN SHALL WE THREE MEET AGAIN? IN THUNDER, LIGHTNING OR IN RAIN?
WHEN THE HURLY-BURLY'S DONE, WHEN THE BATTLE'S LOST AND WON.
WHAT BLOODY MAN IS THAT? HE CAN REPORT.
THIS IS THE SERGEANT.
THE NORWEGIAN LORD, WITH FURBISHED ARMS AND NEW SUPPLIES OF MEN, BEGAN A FRESH ASSAULT.
DISMAYED NOT THIS OUR CAPTAINS, MACBETH AND BANQUO?
I MUST REPORT THEY WERE AS CANNONS OVERCHARGED WITH DOUBLE CRACKS, SO THEY DOUBLY REDOUBLED STROKES UPON THE FOE.

King Duncan of Scotland requests a report of the ongoing battle.

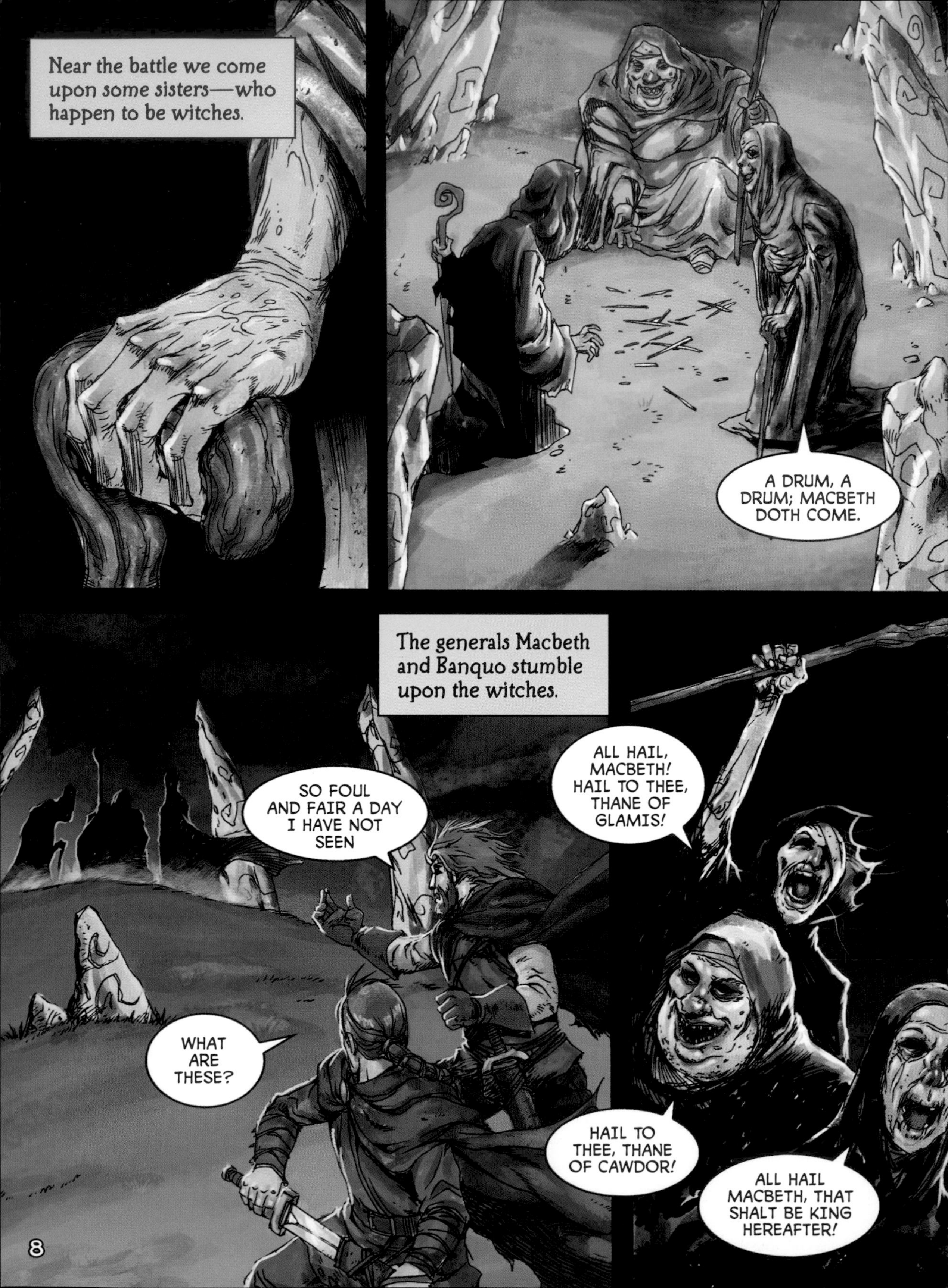
Near the battle we come upon some sisters—who happen to be witches.
A DRUM, A DRUM; MACBETH DOTH COME.
The generals Macbeth and Banquo stumble upon the witches.
SO FOUL AND FAIR A DAY I HAVE NOT SEEN
WHAT ARE THESE?
ALL HAIL, MACBETH! HAIL TO THEE, THANE OF GLAMIS!
HAIL TO THEE, THANE OF CAWDOR!
ALL HAIL MACBETH, THAT SHALT BE KING HEREAFTER!

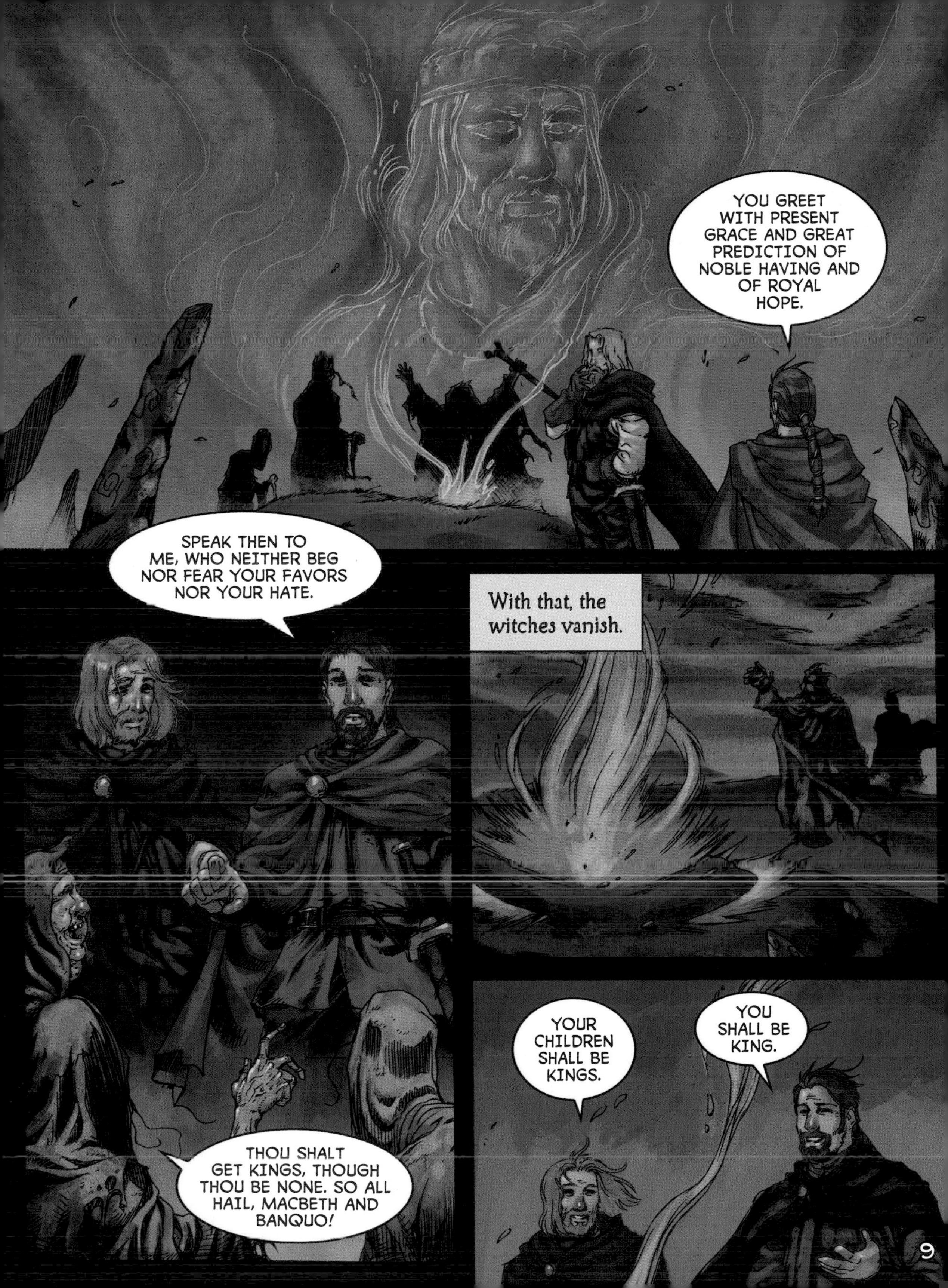
YOU GREET WITH PRESENT GRACE AND GREAT PREDICTION OF NOBLE HAVING AND OF ROYAL HOPE.
SPEAK THEN TO ME, WHO NEITHER BEG NOR FEAR YOUR FAVORS NOR YOUR HATE.
THOU SHALT GET KINGS, THOUGH THOU BE NONE. SO ALL HAIL, MACBETH AND BANQUO!
With that, the witches vanish.
YOU SHALL BE KING.
YOUR CHILDREN SHALL BE KINGS.

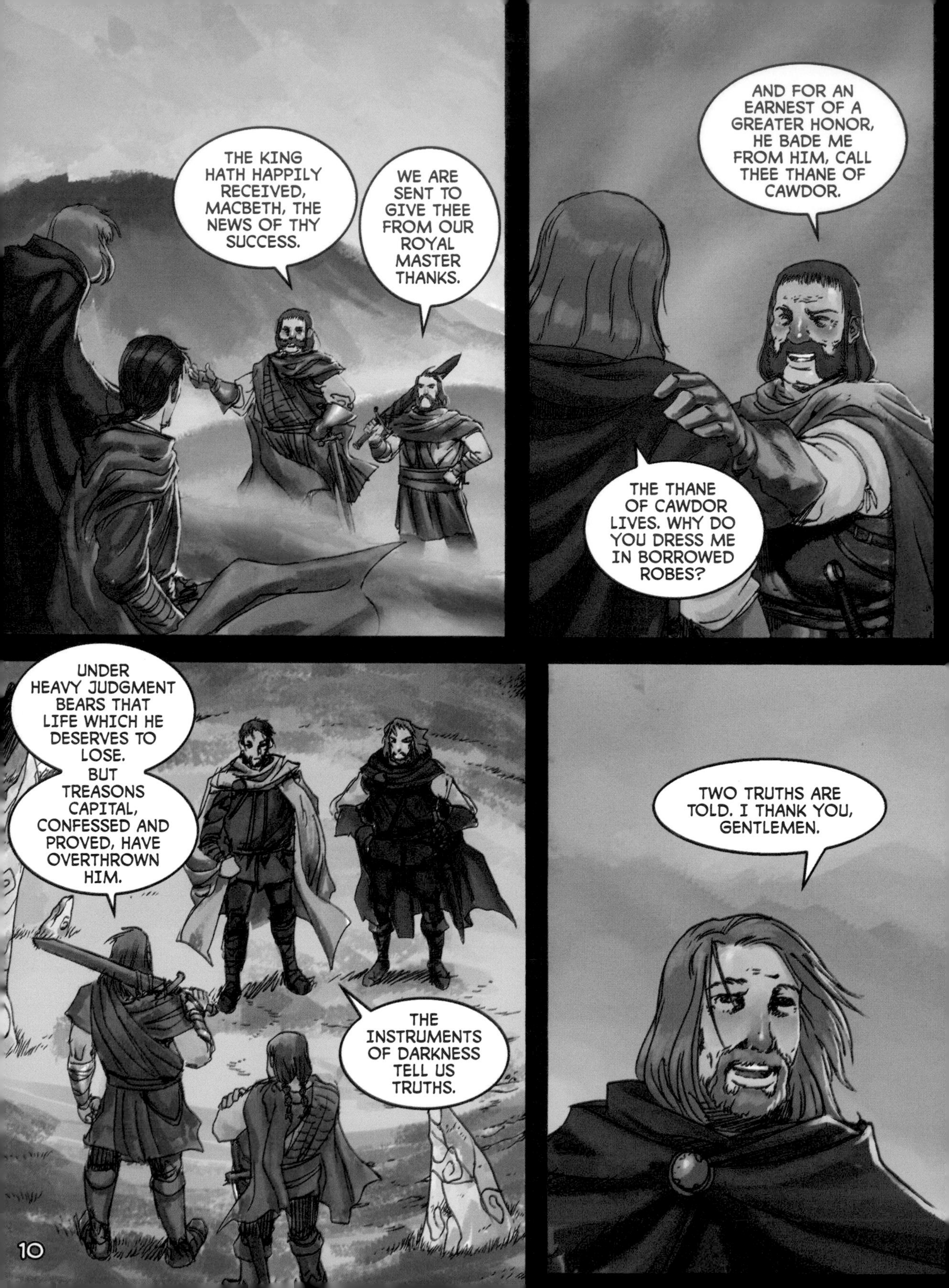
THE KING HATH HAPPILY RECEIVED, MACBETH, THE NEWS OF THY SUCCESS.
WE ARE SENT TO GIVE THEE FROM OUR ROYAL MASTER THANKS.
AND FOR AN EARNEST OF A GREATER HONOR, HE BADE ME FROM HIM, CALL THEE THANE OF CAWDOR.
THE THANE OF CAWDOR LIVES. WHY DO YOU DRESS ME IN BORROWED ROBES?
UNDER HEAVY JUDGMENT BEARS THAT LIFE WHICH HE DESERVES TO LOSE. BUT TREASONS CAPITAL, CONFESSED AND PROVED, HAVE OVERTHROWN HIM.
THE INSTRUMENTS OF DARKNESS TELL US TRUTHS.
TWO TRUTHS ARE TOLD. I THANK YOU, GENTLEMEN.

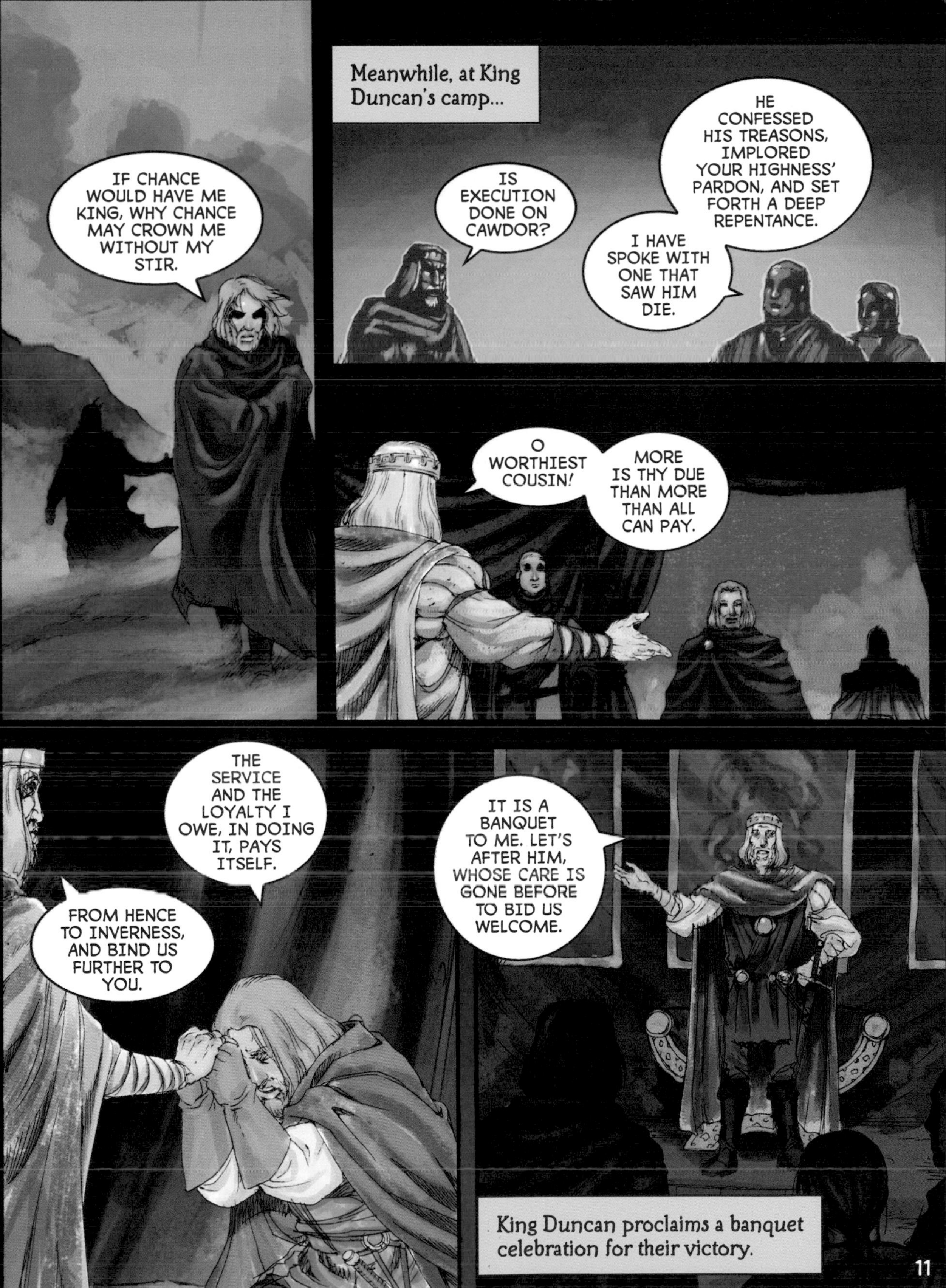

IF CHANCE WOULD HAVE ME KING, WHY CHANCE MAY CROWN ME WITHOUT MY STIR.
Meanwhile, at King Duncan's camp...
IS EXECUTION DONE ON CAWDOR?
HE CONFESSED HIS TREASONS, IMPLORED YOUR HIGHNESS' PARDON, AND SET FORTH A DEEP REPENTANCE.
I HAVE SPOKE WITH ONE THAT SAW HIM DIE.
O WORTHIEST COUSIN!
MORE IS THY DUE THAN MORE THAN ALL CAN PAY.
THE SERVICE AND THE LOYALTY I OWE, IN DOING IT, PAYS ITSELF.
FROM HENCE TO INVERNESS, AND BIND US FURTHER TO YOU.
IT IS A BANQUET TO ME. LET'S AFTER HIM, WHOSE CARE IS GONE BEFORE TO BID US WELCOME.
King Duncan proclaims a banquet celebration for their victory.

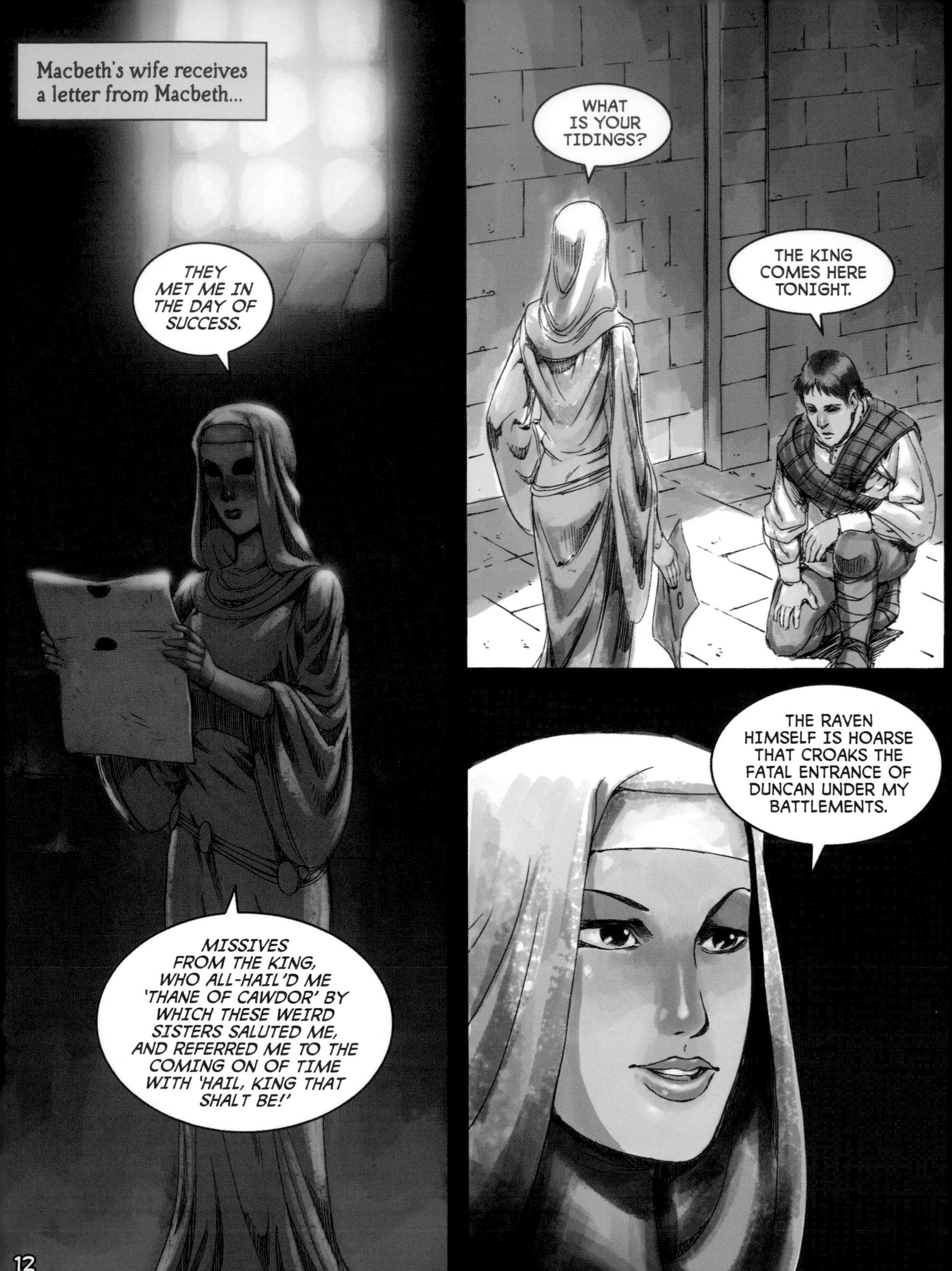

Macbeth's wife receives a letter from Macbeth...
THEY MET ME IN THE DAY OF SUCCESS.
MISSIVES FROM THE KING, WHO ALL-HAIL'D ME 'THANE OF CAWDOR' BY WHICH THESE WEIRD SISTERS SALUTED ME, AND REFERRED ME TO THE COMING ON OF TIME WITH 'HAIL, KING THAT SHALT BE!'
WHAT IS YOUR TIDINGS?
THE KING COMES HERE TONIGHT.
THE RAVEN HIMSELF IS HOARSE THAT CROAKS THE FATAL ENTRANCE OF DUNCAN UNDER MY BATTLEMENTS.

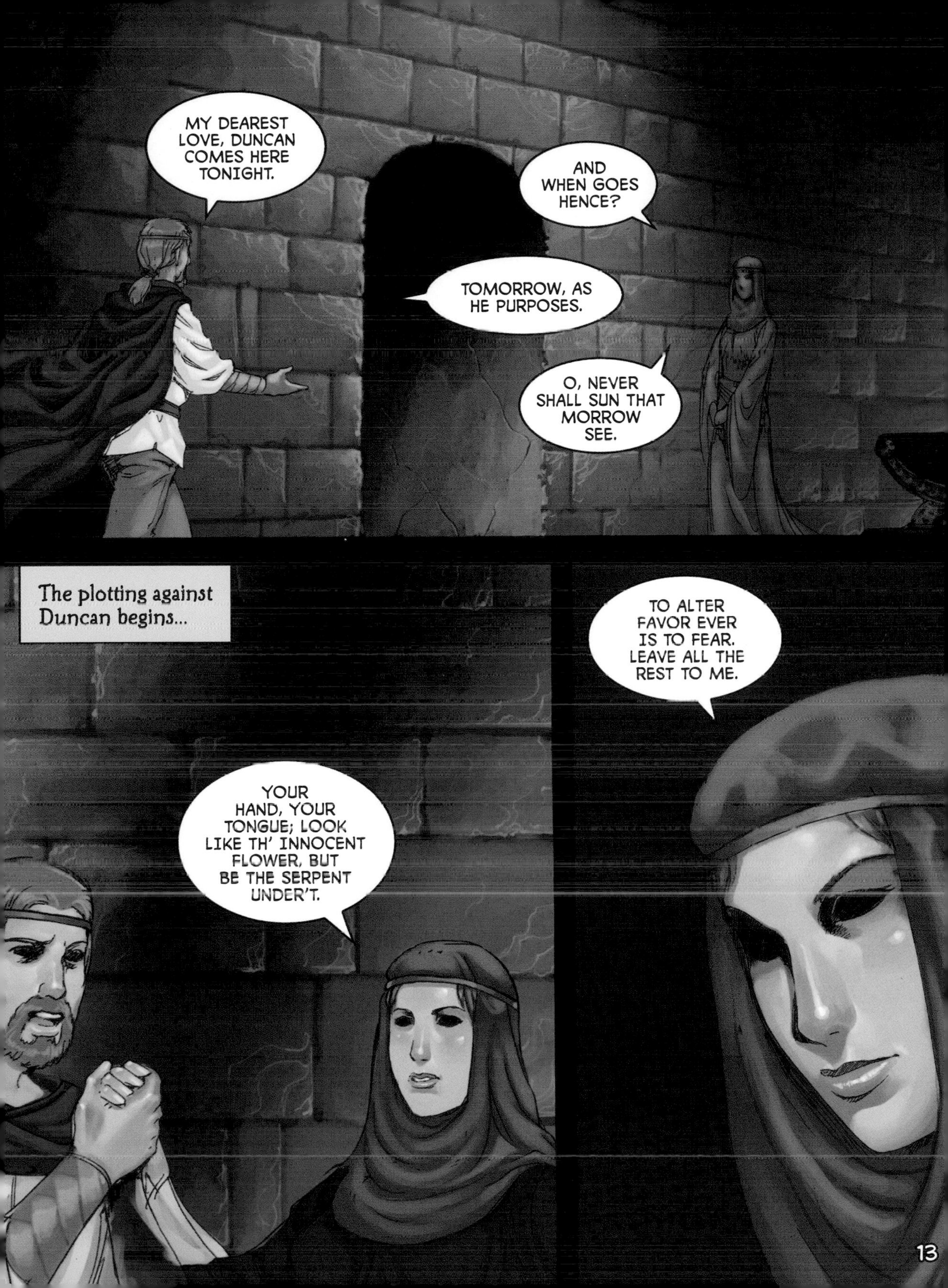
MY DEAREST LOVE, DUNCAN COMES HERE TONIGHT.
AND WHEN GOES HENCE?
TOMORROW, AS HE PURPOSES.
O, NEVER SHALL SUN THAT MORROW SEE.
The plotting against Duncan begins...
YOUR HAND, YOUR TONGUE; LOOK LIKE TH' INNOCENT FLOWER, BUT BE THE SERPENT UNDER'T.
TO ALTER FAVOR EVER IS TO FEAR. LEAVE ALL THE REST TO ME.

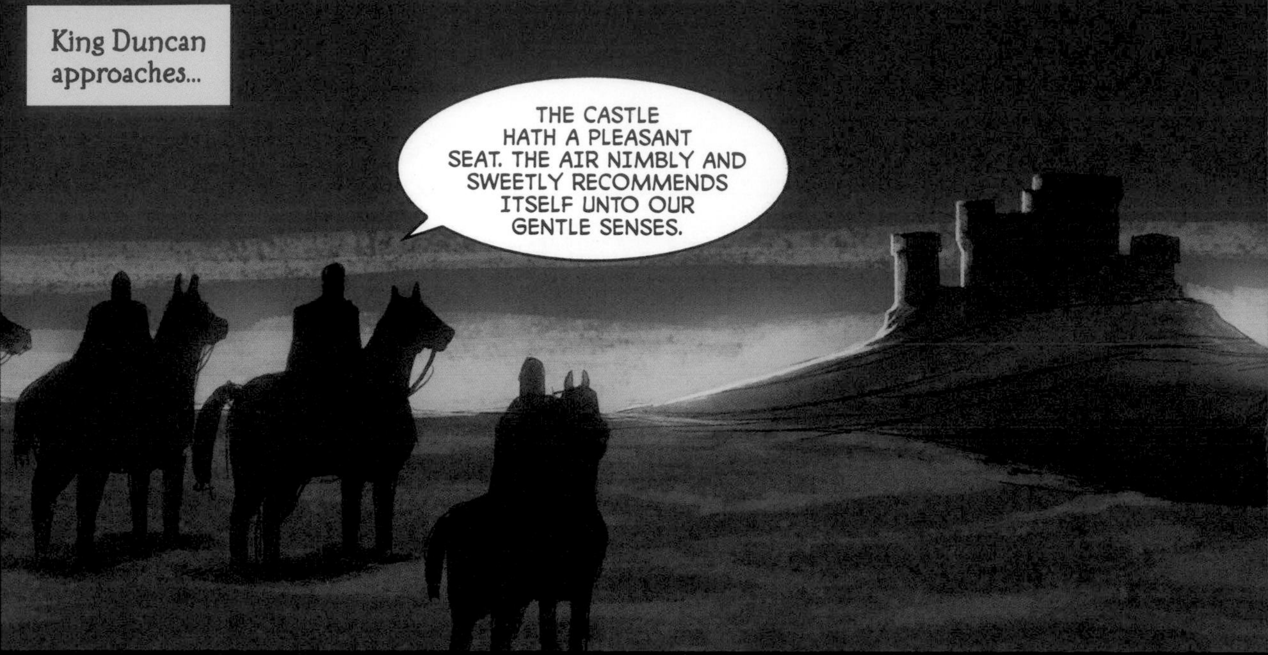
King Duncan approaches...
THE CASTLE HATH A PLEASANT SEAT. THE AIR NIMBLY AND SWEETLY RECOMMENDS ITSELF UNTO OUR GENTLE SENSES.

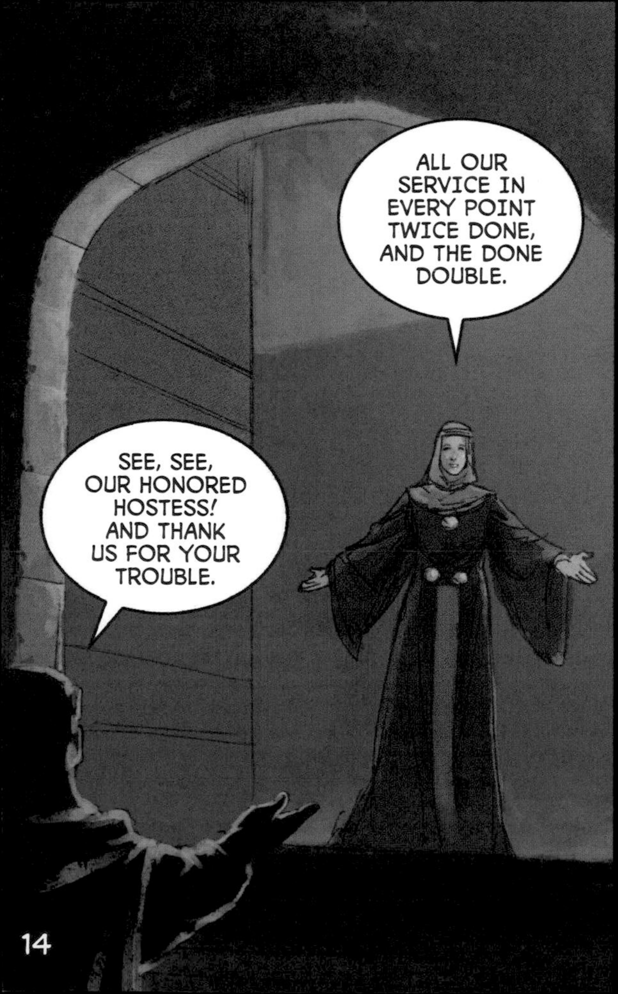
SEE, SEE, OUR HONORED HOSTESS! AND THANK US FOR YOUR TROUBLE.
ALL OUR SERVICE IN EVERY POINT TWICE DONE, AND THE DONE DOUBLE.

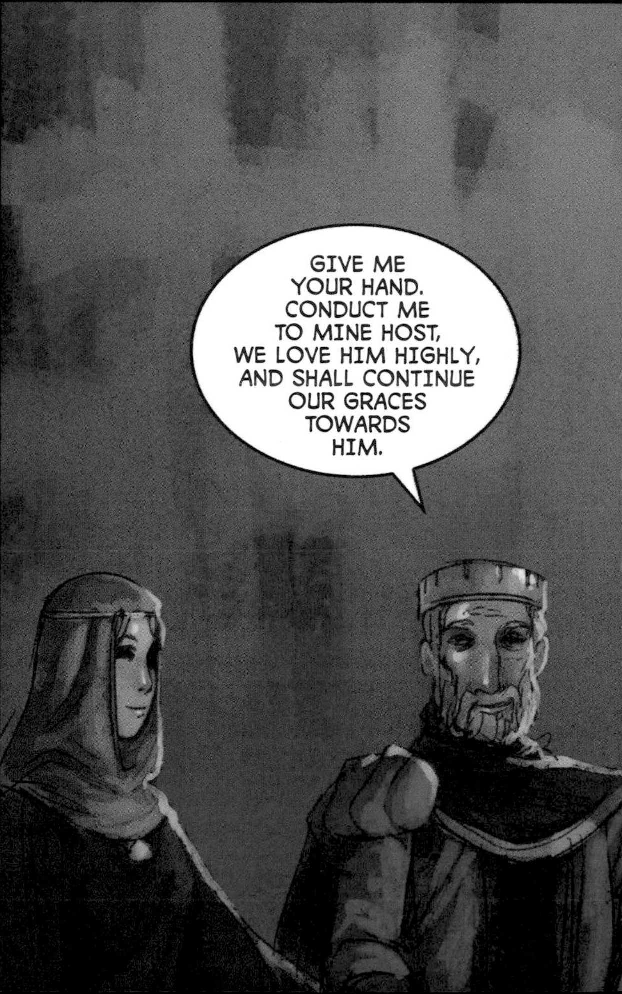
GIVE ME YOUR HAND. CONDUCT ME TO MINE HOST, WE LOVE HIM HIGHLY, AND SHALL CONTINUE OUR GRACES TOWARDS HIM.

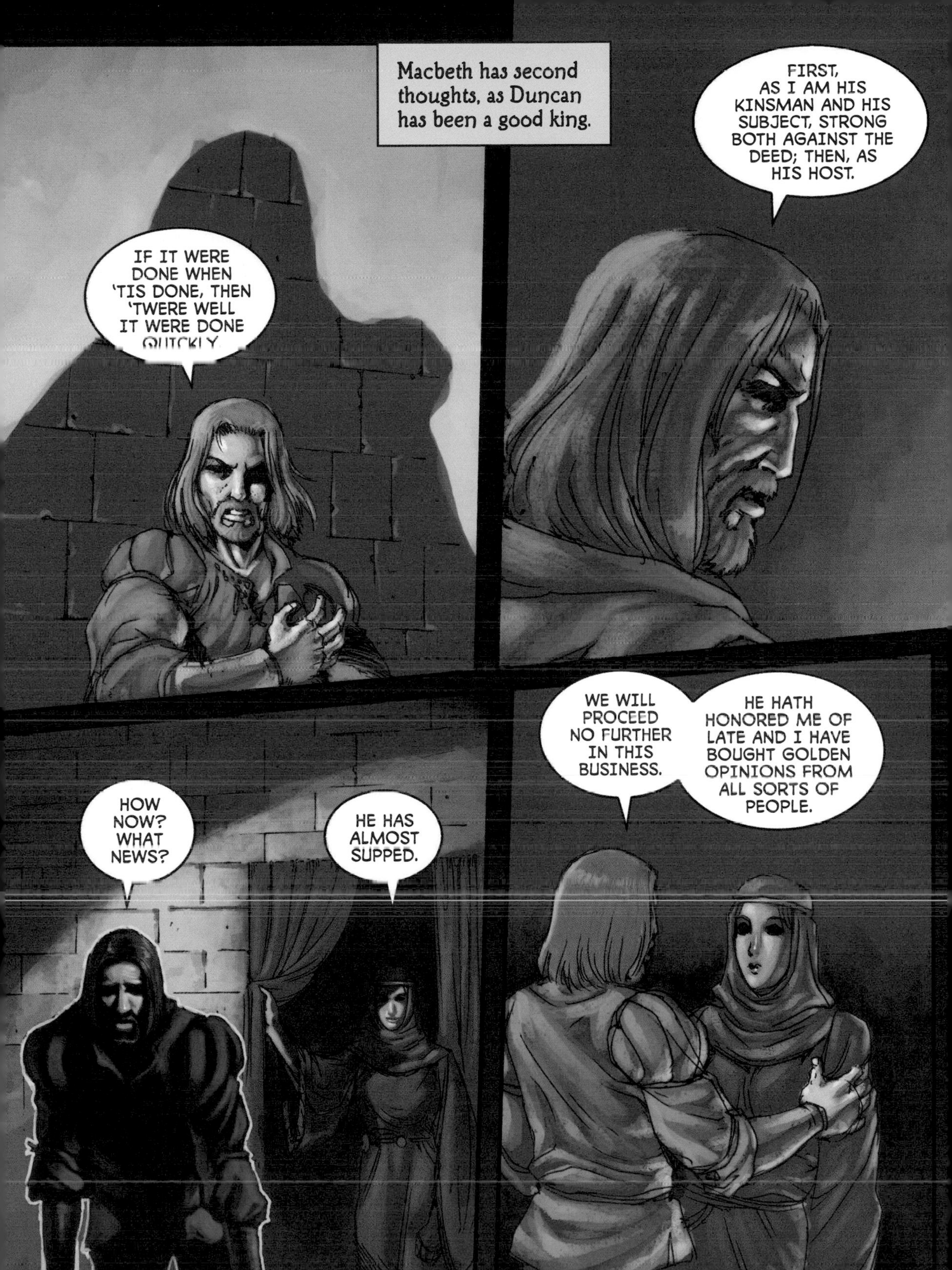

Macbeth has second thoughts, as Duncan has been a good king.
IF IT WERE DONE WHEN 'TIS DONE, THEN 'TWERE WELL IT WERE DONE QUICKLY.
FIRST, AS I AM HIS KINSMAN AND HIS SUBJECT, STRONG BOTH AGAINST THE DEED; THEN, AS HIS HOST.
HOW NOW? WHAT NEWS?
HE HAS ALMOST SUPPED.
WE WILL PROCEED NO FURTHER IN THIS BUSINESS.
HE HATH HONORED ME OF LATE AND I HAVE BOUGHT GOLDEN OPINIONS FROM ALL SORTS OF PEOPLE.

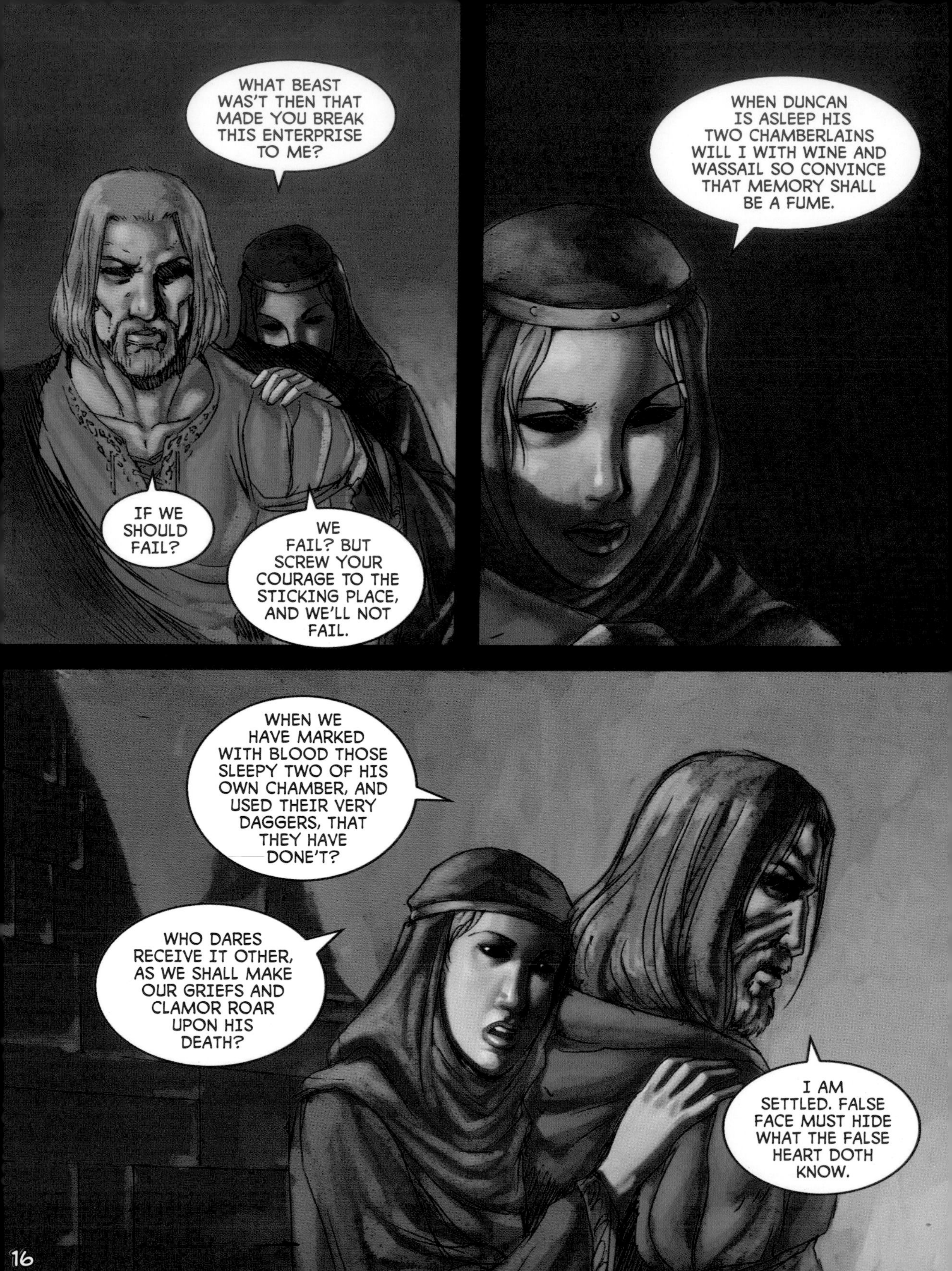
WHAT BEAST WAS'T THEN THAT MADE YOU BREAK THIS ENTERPRISE TO ME?
IF WE SHOULD FAIL?
WE FAIL? BUT SCREW YOUR COURAGE TO THE STICKING PLACE, AND WE'LL NOT FAIL.
WHEN DUNCAN IS ASLEEP HIS TWO CHAMBERLAINS WILL I WITH WINE AND WASSAIL SO CONVINCE THAT MEMORY SHALL BE A FUME.
WHEN WE HAVE MARKED WITH BLOOD THOSE SLEEPY TWO OF HIS OWN CHAMBER, AND USED THEIR VERY DAGGERS, THAT THEY HAVE DONE'T?
WHO DARES RECEIVE IT OTHER, AS WE SHALL MAKE OUR GRIEFS AND CLAMOR ROAR UPON HIS DEATH?
I AM SETTLED. FALSE FACE MUST HIDE WHAT THE FALSE HEART DOTH KNOW.

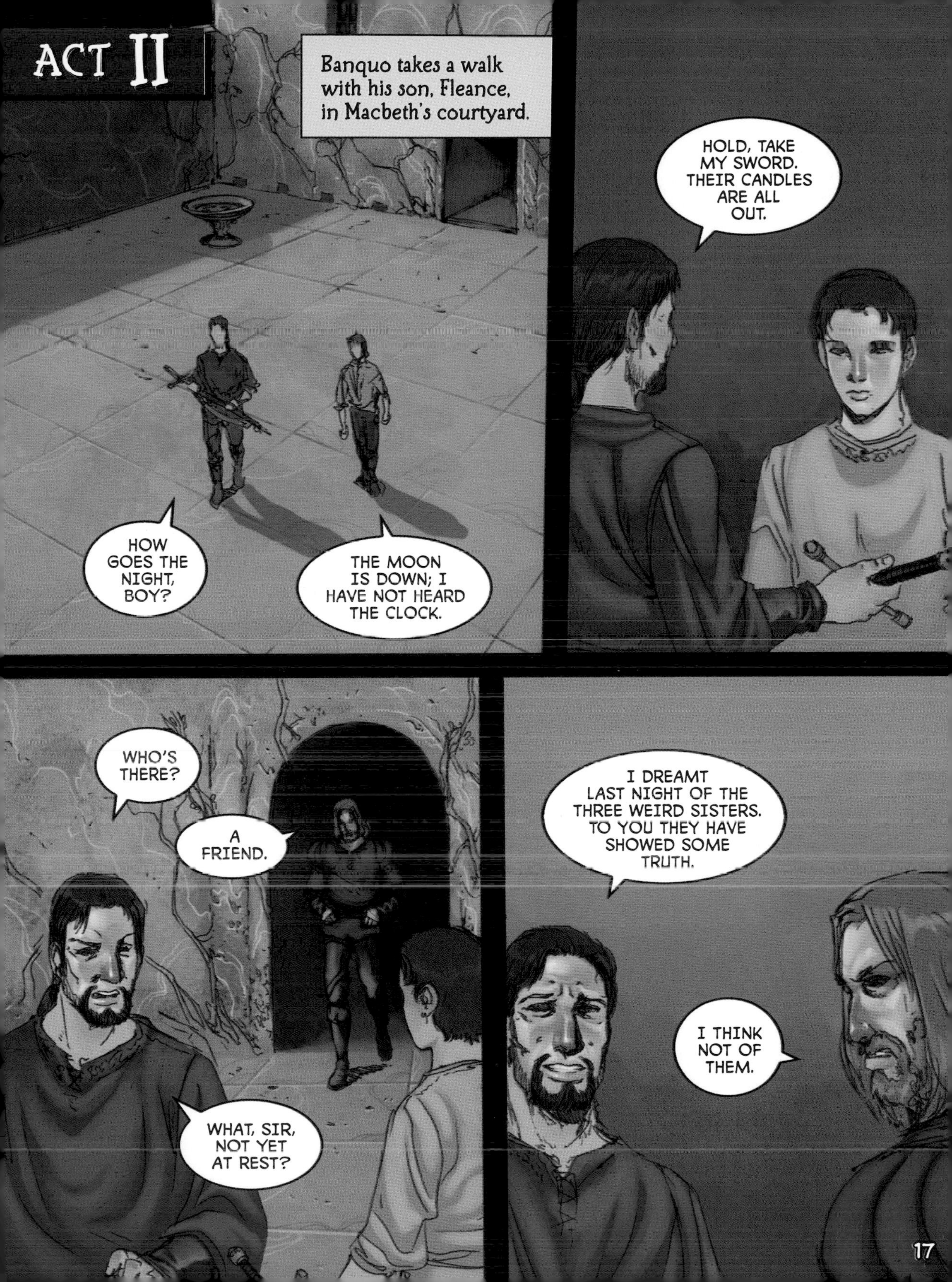
ACT II
Banquo takes a walk with his son, Fleance, in Macbeth's courtyard.
HOW GOES THE NIGHT, BOY?
THE MOON IS DOWN; I HAVE NOT HEARD THE CLOCK.
HOLD, TAKE MY SWORD. THEIR CANDLES ARE ALL OUT.
WHO'S THERE?
A FRIEND.
WHAT, SIR, NOT YET AT REST?
I DREAMT LAST NIGHT OF THE THREE WEIRD SISTERS. TO YOU THEY HAVE SHOWED SOME TRUTH.
I THINK NOT OF THEM.

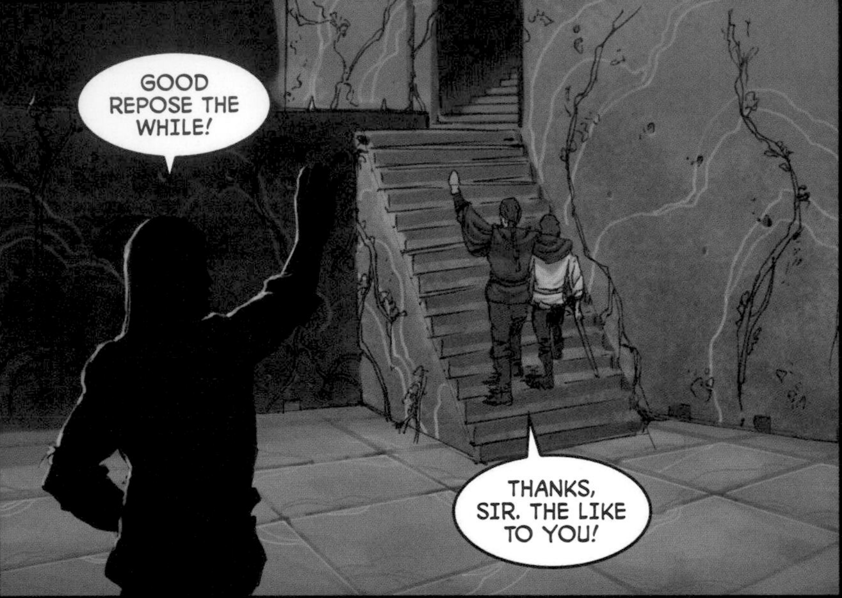
GOOD REPOSE THE WHILE!
THANKS, SIR. THE LIKE TO YOU!

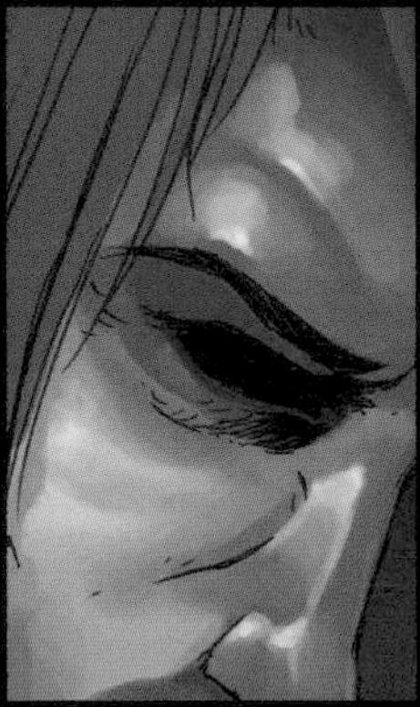

Macbeth thinks about the act he is about to perform.

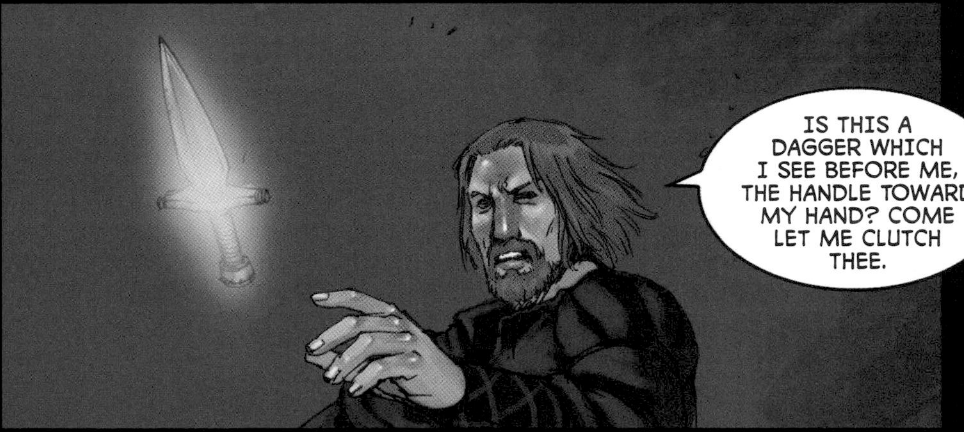
IS THIS A DAGGER WHICH I SEE BEFORE ME, THE HANDLE TOWARD MY HAND? COME LET ME CLUTCH THEE.

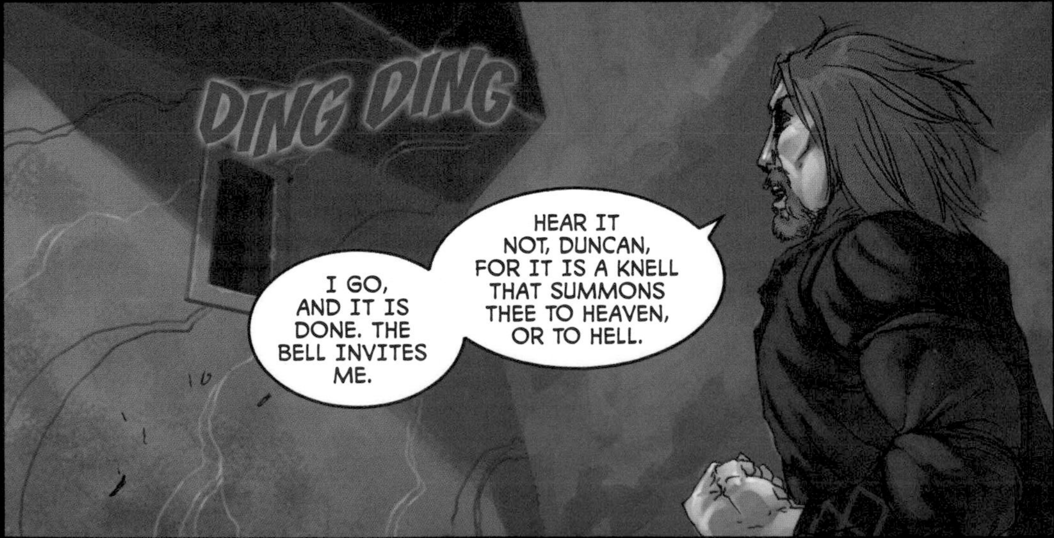
DING DING
I GO, AND IT IS DONE. THE BELL INVITES ME.
HEAR IT NOT, DUNCAN, FOR IT IS A KNELL THAT SUMMONS THEE TO HEAVEN, OR TO HELL.

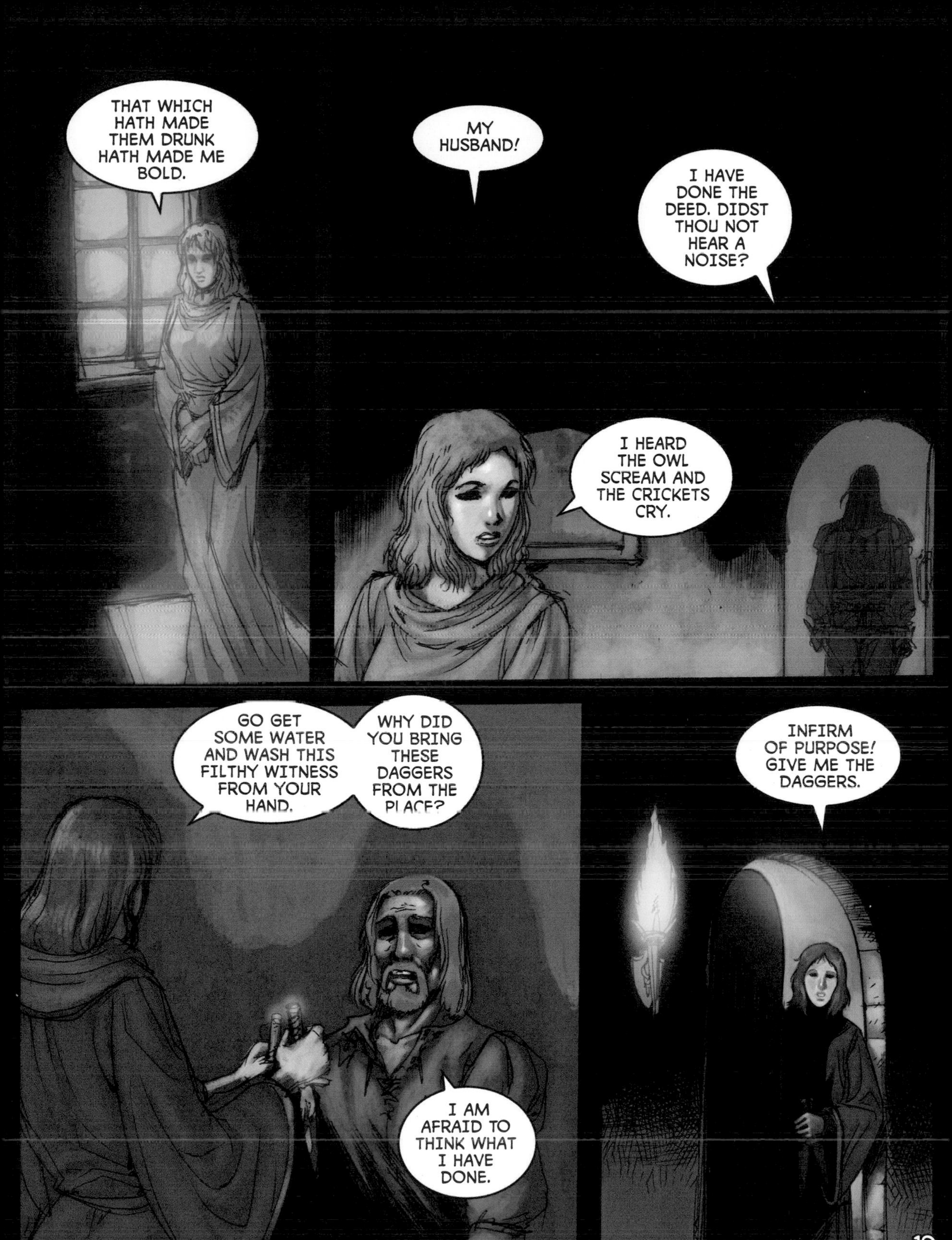

THAT WHICH HATH MADE THEM DRUNK HATH MADE ME BOLD.
MY HUSBAND!
I HAVE DONE THE DEED. DIDST THOU NOT HEAR A NOISE?
I HEARD THE OWL SCREAM AND THE CRICKETS CRY.
GO GET SOME WATER AND WASH THIS FILTHY WITNESS FROM YOUR HAND.
WHY DID YOU BRING THESE DAGGERS FROM THE PLACE?
I AM AFRAID TO THINK WHAT I HAVE DONE.
INFIRM OF PURPOSE! GIVE ME THE DAGGERS.

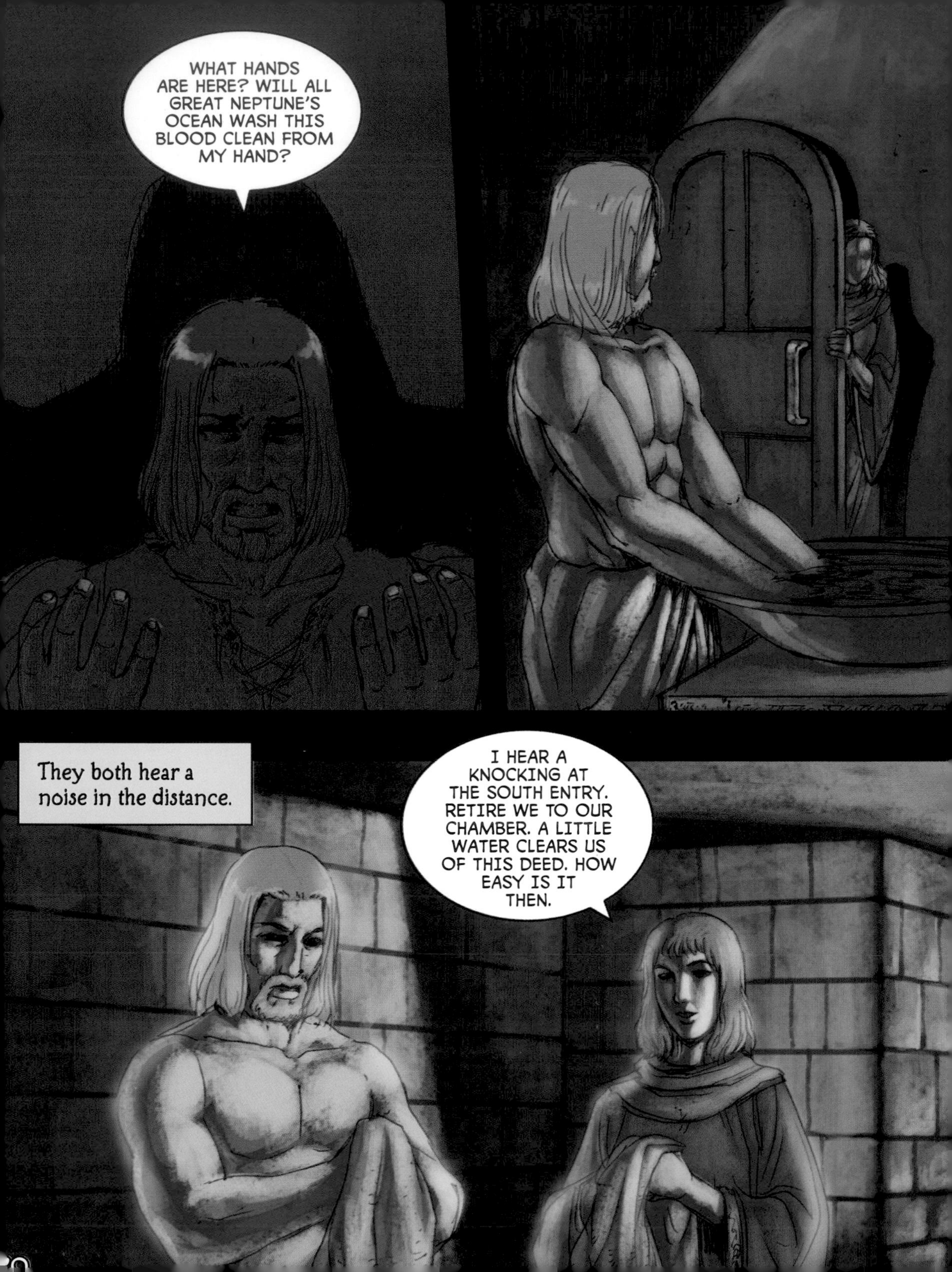
WHAT HANDS ARE HERE? WILL ALL GREAT NEPTUNE'S OCEAN WASH THIS BLOOD CLEAN FROM MY HAND?
They both hear a noise in the distance.
I HEAR A KNOCKING AT THE SOUTH ENTRY. RETIRE WE TO OUR CHAMBER. A LITTLE WATER CLEARS US OF THIS DEED. HOW EASY IS IT THEN.

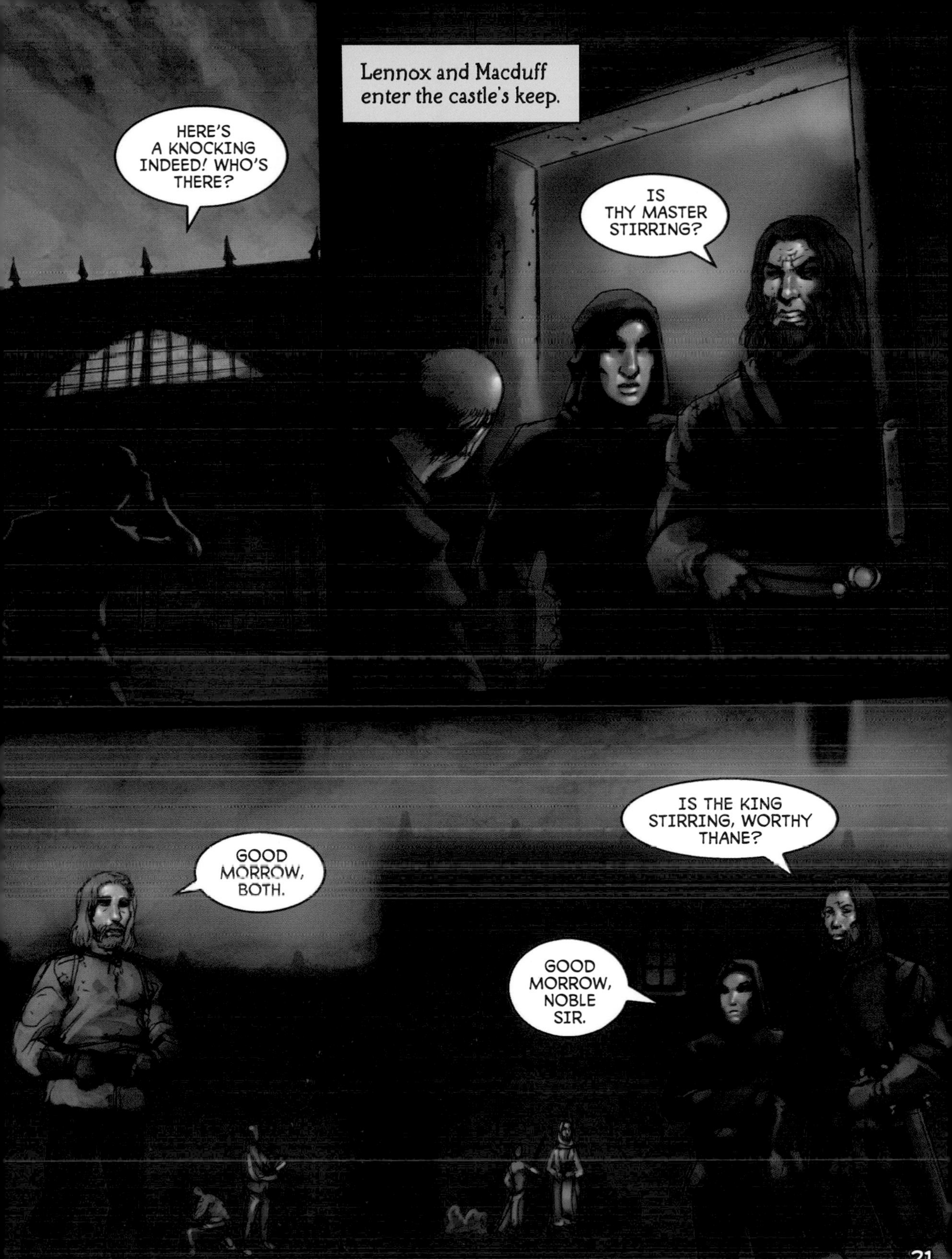
Lennox and Macduff enter the castle's keep.
HERE'S A KNOCKING INDEED! WHO'S THERE?
IS THY MASTER STIRRING?
GOOD MORROW, BOTH.
IS THE KING STIRRING, WORTHY THANE?
GOOD MORROW, NOBLE SIR.

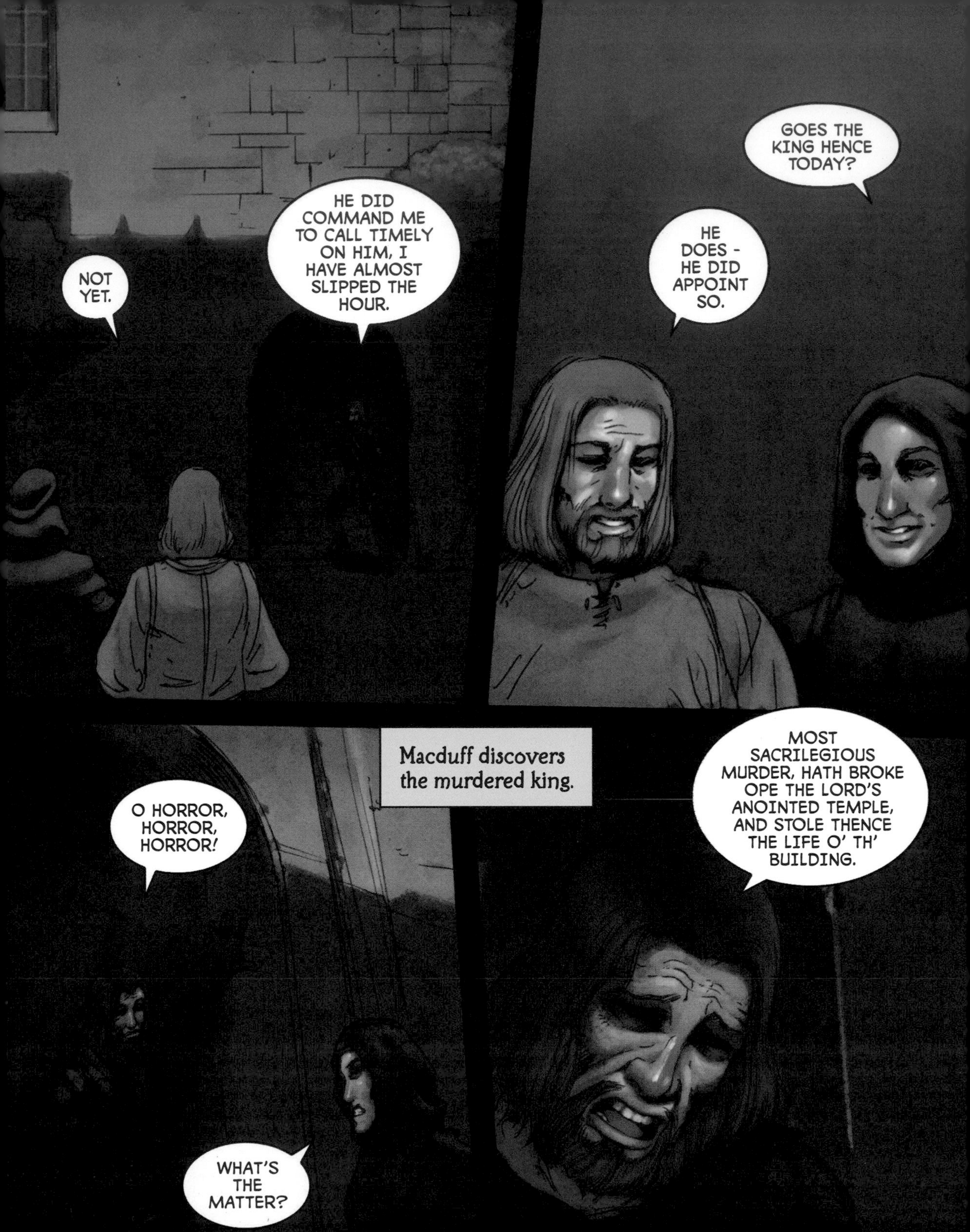
NOT YET.
HE DID COMMAND ME TO CALL TIMELY ON HIM, I HAVE ALMOST SLIPPED THE HOUR.
GOES THE KING HENCE TODAY?
HE DOES - HE DID APPOINT SO.
Macduff discovers the murdered king.
O HORROR, HORROR, HORROR!
WHAT'S THE MATTER?
MOST SACRILEGIOUS MURDER, HATH BROKE OPE THE LORD'S ANOINTED TEMPLE, AND STOLE THENCE THE LIFE O' TH' BUILDING.

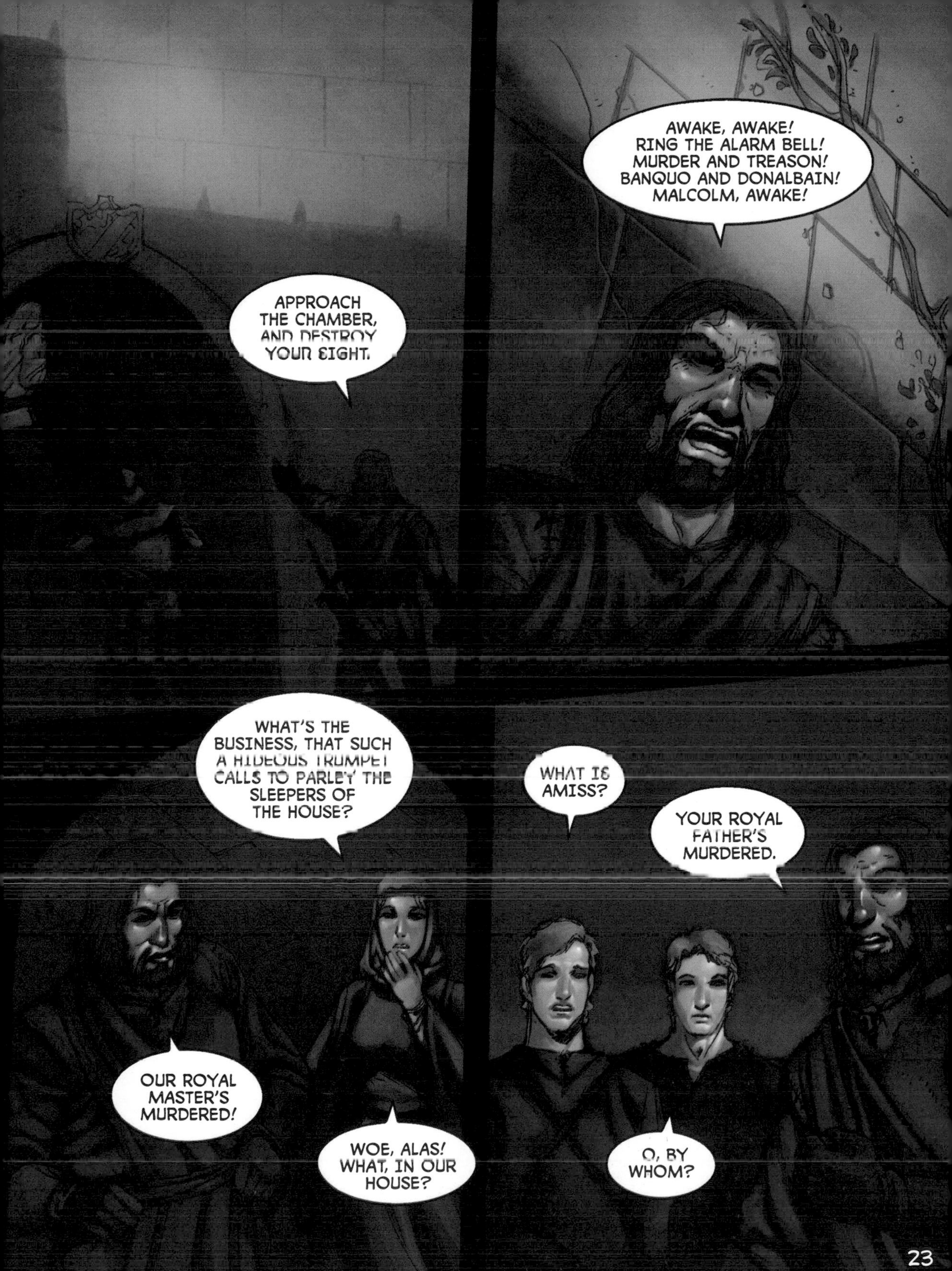
APPROACH THE CHAMBER, AND DESTROY YOUR SIGHT.
AWAKE, AWAKE! RING THE ALARM BELL! MURDER AND TREASON! BANQUO AND DONALBAIN! MALCOLM, AWAKE!
WHAT'S THE BUSINESS, THAT SUCH A HIDEOUS TRUMPET CALLS TO PARLEY THE SLEEPERS OF THE HOUSE?
OUR ROYAL MASTER'S MURDERED!
WOE, ALAS! WHAT, IN OUR HOUSE?
WHAT IS AMISS?
YOUR ROYAL FATHER'S MURDERED.
O, BY WHOM?

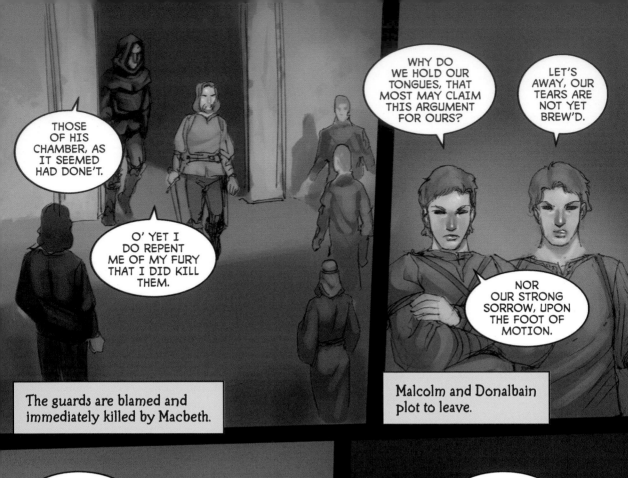

THOSE OF HIS CHAMBER, AS IT SEEMED HAD DONE'T.

O' YET I DO REPENT ME OF MY FURY THAT I DID KILL THEM.

WHY DO WE HOLD OUR TONGUES, THAT MOST MAY CLAIM THIS ARGUMENT FOR OURS?

LET'S AWAY, OUR TEARS ARE NOT YET BREW'D.

NOR OUR STRONG SORROW, UPON THE FOOT OF MOTION.

The guards are blamed and immediately killed by Macbeth.

Malcolm and Donalbain plot to leave.

LET US MEET AND QUESTION THIS MOST BLOODY PIECE OF WORK.

LET'S BRIEFLY PUT ON MANLY READINESS, AND MEET I' TH' HALL TOGETHER.

Banquo calls all the nobles together to discuss their king's murder.

LET'S NOT CONSORT WITH THEM. I'LL TO ENGLAND.

TO IRELAND I. OUR SEPARATED FORTUNE SHALL KEEP US BOTH THE SAFER.

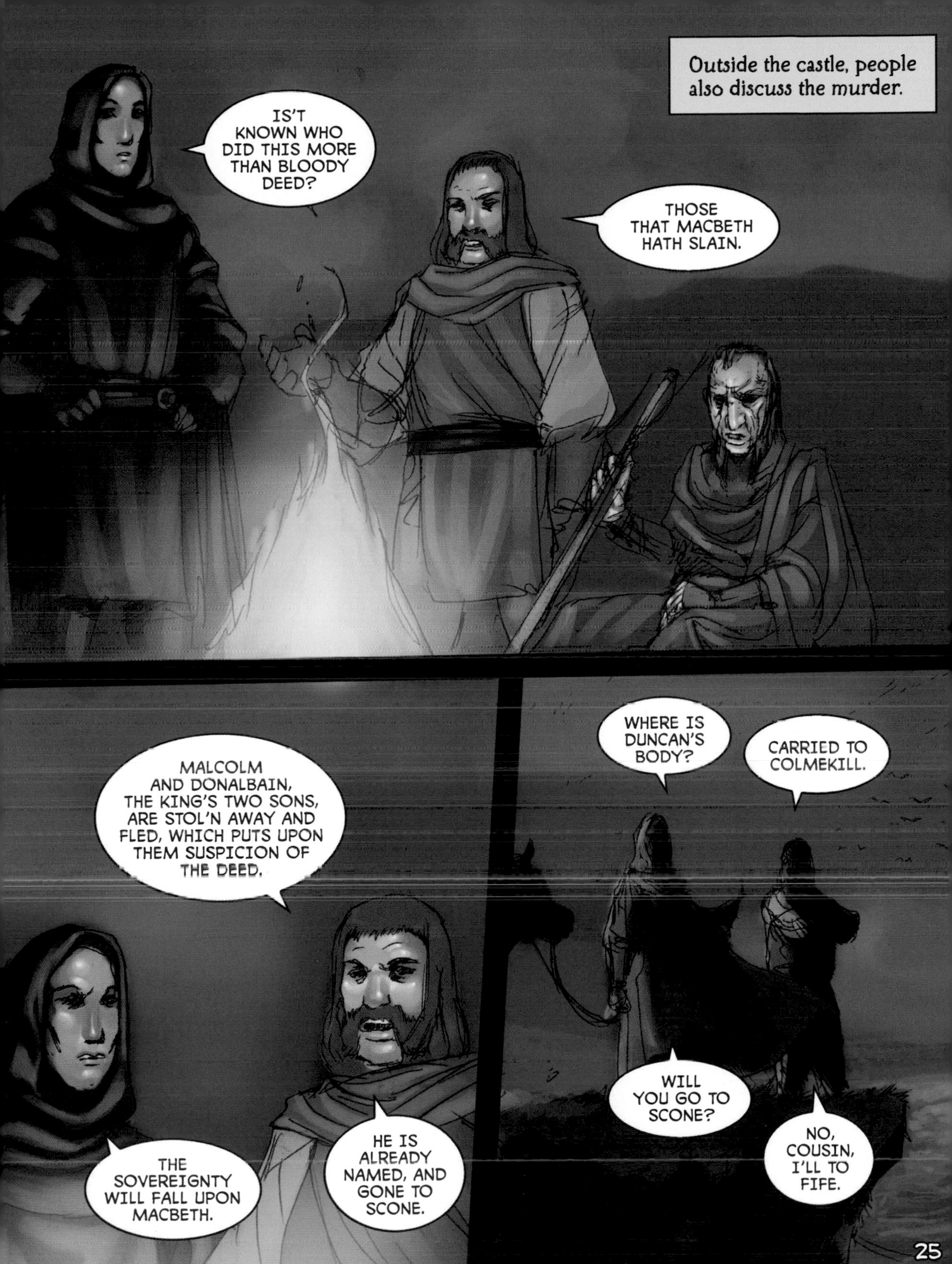

Outside the castle, people also discuss the murder.
IS'T KNOWN WHO DID THIS MORE THAN BLOODY DEED?
THOSE THAT MACBETH HATH SLAIN.
MALCOLM AND DONALBAIN, THE KING'S TWO SONS, ARE STOL'N AWAY AND FLED, WHICH PUTS UPON THEM SUSPICION OF THE DEED.
THE SOVEREIGNTY WILL FALL UPON MACBETH.
HE IS ALREADY NAMED, AND GONE TO SCONE.
WHERE IS DUNCAN'S BODY?
CARRIED TO COLMEKILL.
WILL YOU GO TO SCONE?
NO, COUSIN, I'LL TO FIFE.

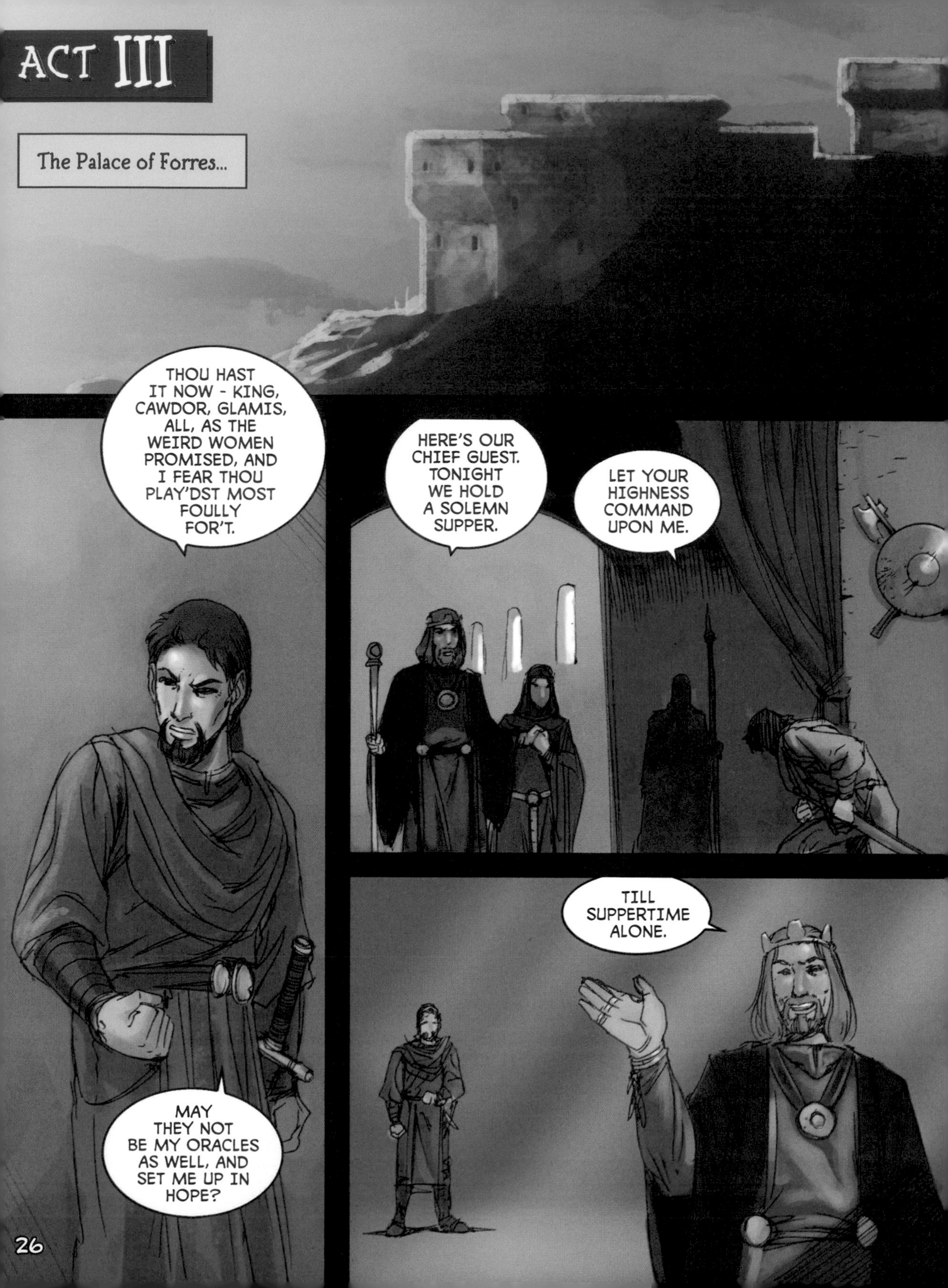
ACT III
The Palace of Forres...
THOU HAST IT NOW - KING, CAWDOR, GLAMIS, ALL, AS THE WEIRD WOMEN PROMISED, AND I FEAR THOU PLAY'DST MOST FOULLY FOR'T.
HERE'S OUR CHIEF GUEST. TONIGHT WE HOLD A SOLEMN SUPPER.
LET YOUR HIGHNESS COMMAND UPON ME.
TILL SUPPERTIME ALONE.
MAY THEY NOT BE MY ORACLES AS WELL, AND SET ME UP IN HOPE?

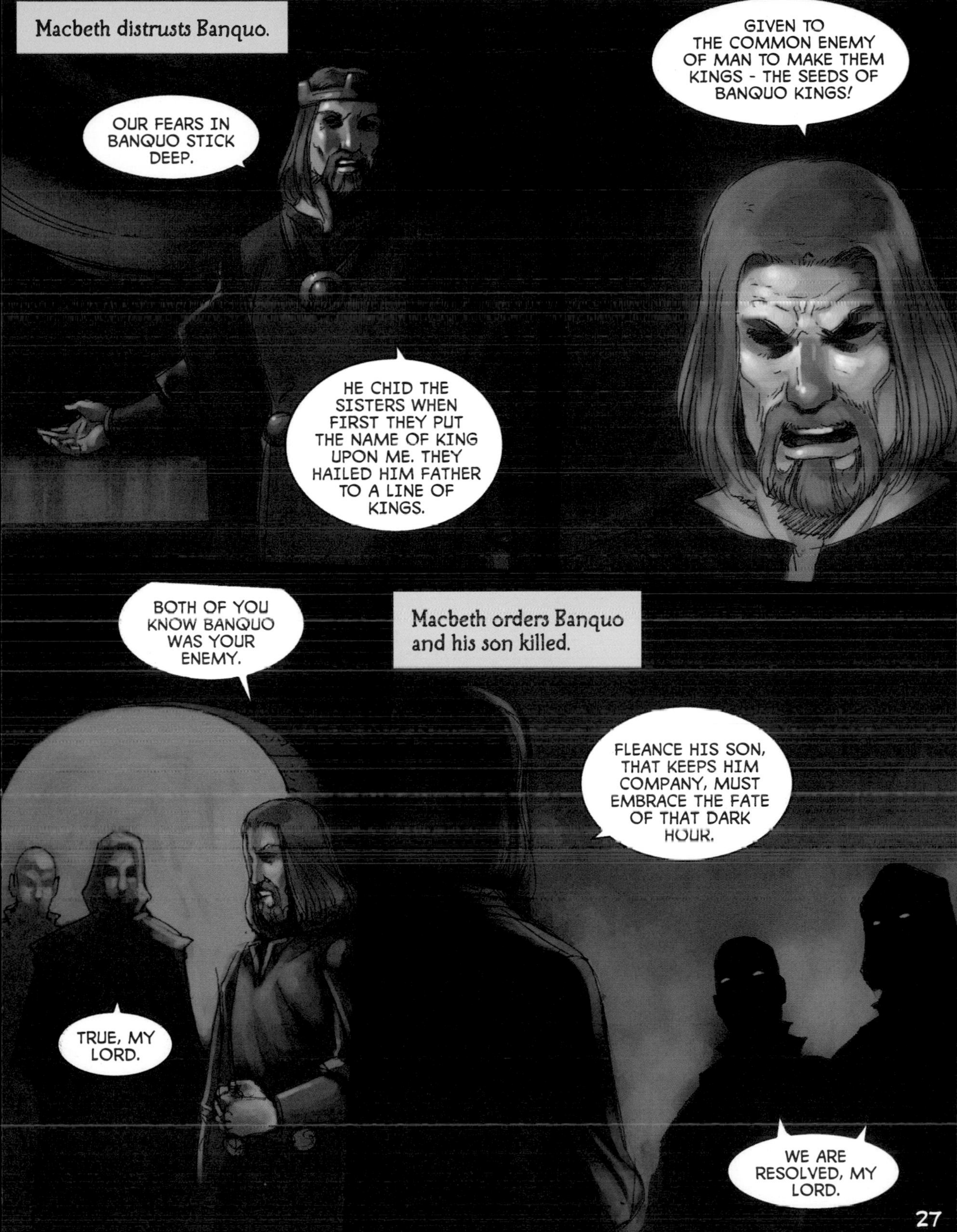
Macbeth distrusts Banquo.
OUR FEARS IN BANQUO STICK DEEP.
HE CHID THE SISTERS WHEN FIRST THEY PUT THE NAME OF KING UPON ME. THEY HAILED HIM FATHER TO A LINE OF KINGS.
GIVEN TO THE COMMON ENEMY OF MAN TO MAKE THEM KINGS - THE SEEDS OF BANQUO KINGS!
Macbeth orders Banquo and his son killed.
BOTH OF YOU KNOW BANQUO WAS YOUR ENEMY.
TRUE, MY LORD.
FLEANCE HIS SON, THAT KEEPS HIM COMPANY, MUST EMBRACE THE FATE OF THAT DARK HOUR.
WE ARE RESOLVED, MY LORD.

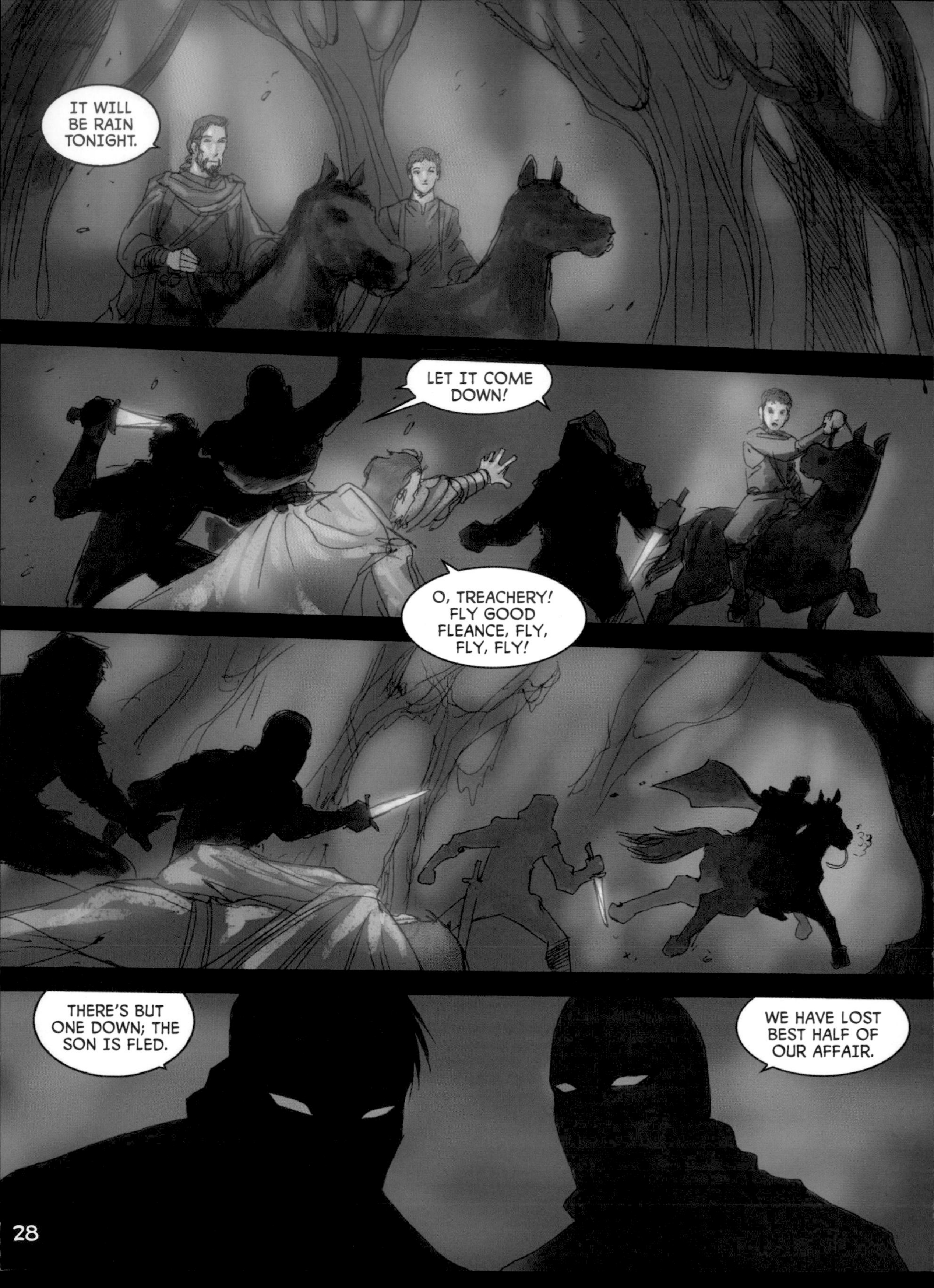
IT WILL BE RAIN TONIGHT.
LET IT COME DOWN!
O, TREACHERY! FLY GOOD FLEANCE, FLY, FLY, FLY!
THERE'S BUT ONE DOWN; THE SON IS FLED.
WE HAVE LOST BEST HALF OF OUR AFFAIR.

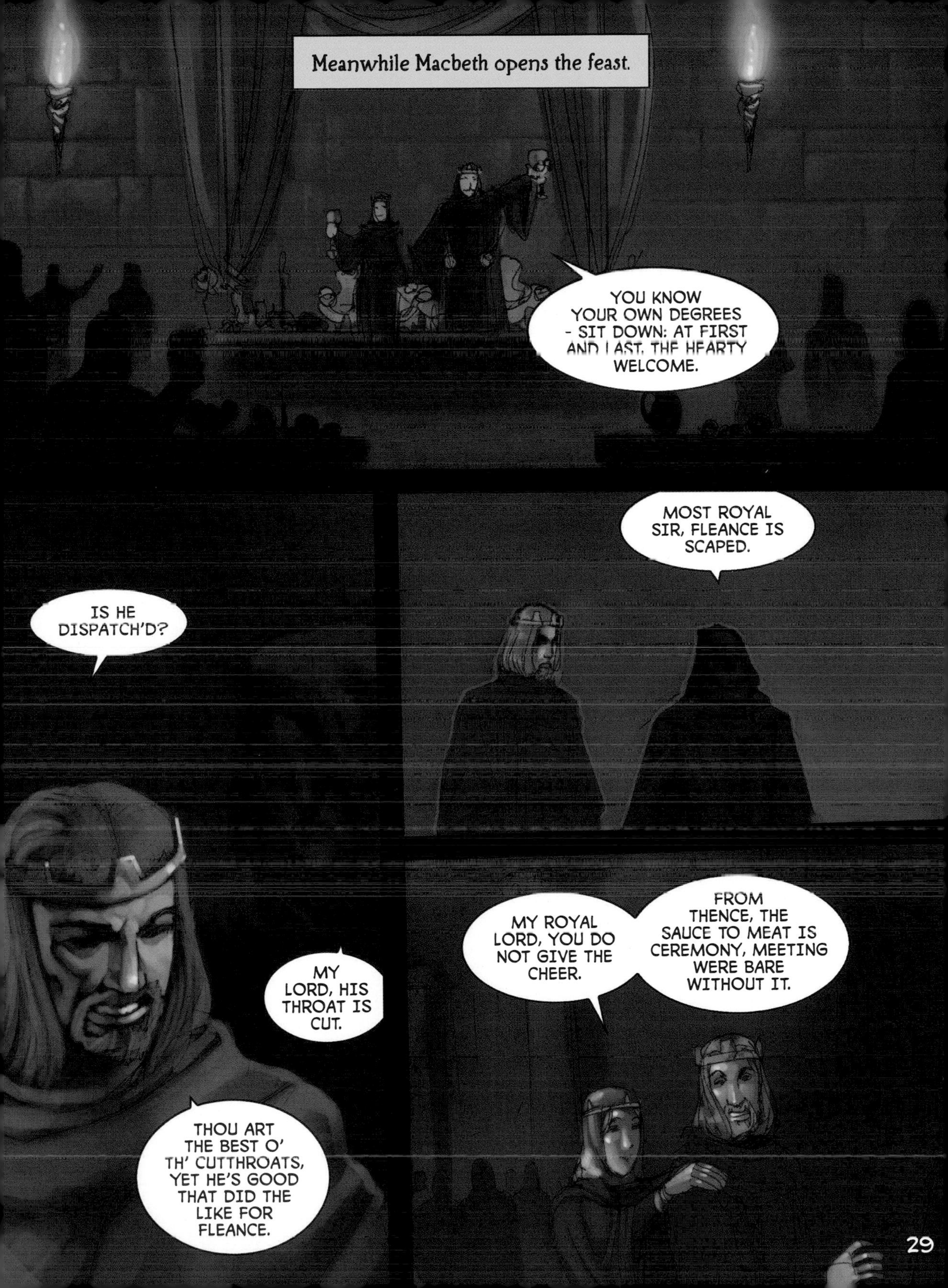
Meanwhile Macbeth opens the feast.
YOU KNOW YOUR OWN DEGREES - SIT DOWN: AT FIRST AND LAST, THE HEARTY WELCOME.
MOST ROYAL SIR, FLEANCE IS SCAPED.
IS HE DISPATCH'D?
MY LORD, HIS THROAT IS CUT.
THOU ART THE BEST O' TH' CUTTHROATS, YET HE'S GOOD THAT DID THE LIKE FOR FLEANCE.
MY ROYAL LORD, YOU DO NOT GIVE THE CHEER.
FROM THENCE, THE SAUCE TO MEAT IS CEREMONY, MEETING WERE BARE WITHOUT IT.

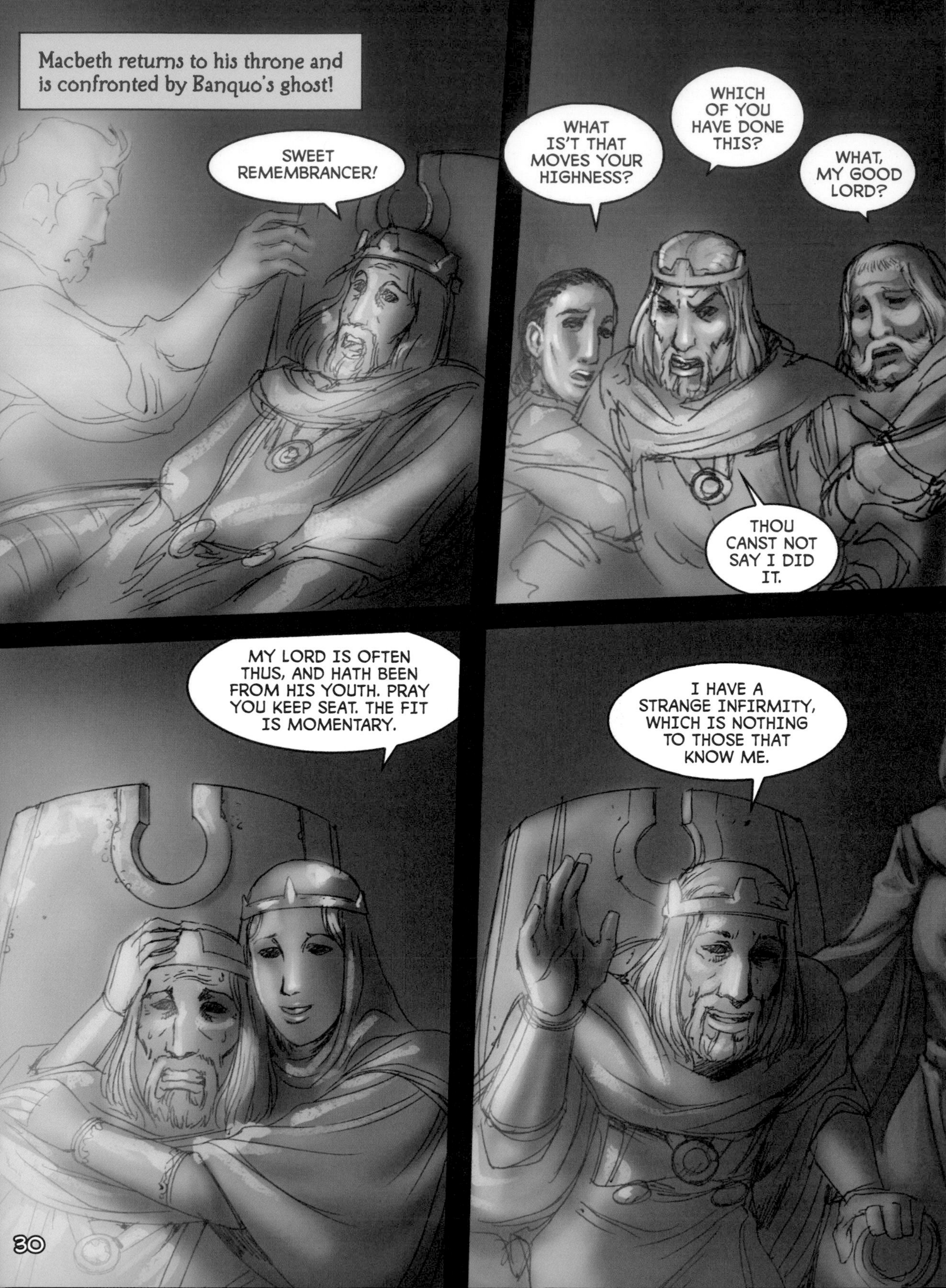
Macbeth returns to his throne and is confronted by Banquo's ghost!
SWEET REMEMBRANCER!
WHAT IS'T THAT MOVES YOUR HIGHNESS?
WHICH OF YOU HAVE DONE THIS?
WHAT, MY GOOD LORD?
THOU CANST NOT SAY I DID IT.
MY LORD IS OFTEN THUS, AND HATH BEEN FROM HIS YOUTH. PRAY YOU KEEP SEAT. THE FIT IS MOMENTARY.
I HAVE A STRANGE INFIRMITY, WHICH IS NOTHING TO THOSE THAT KNOW ME.

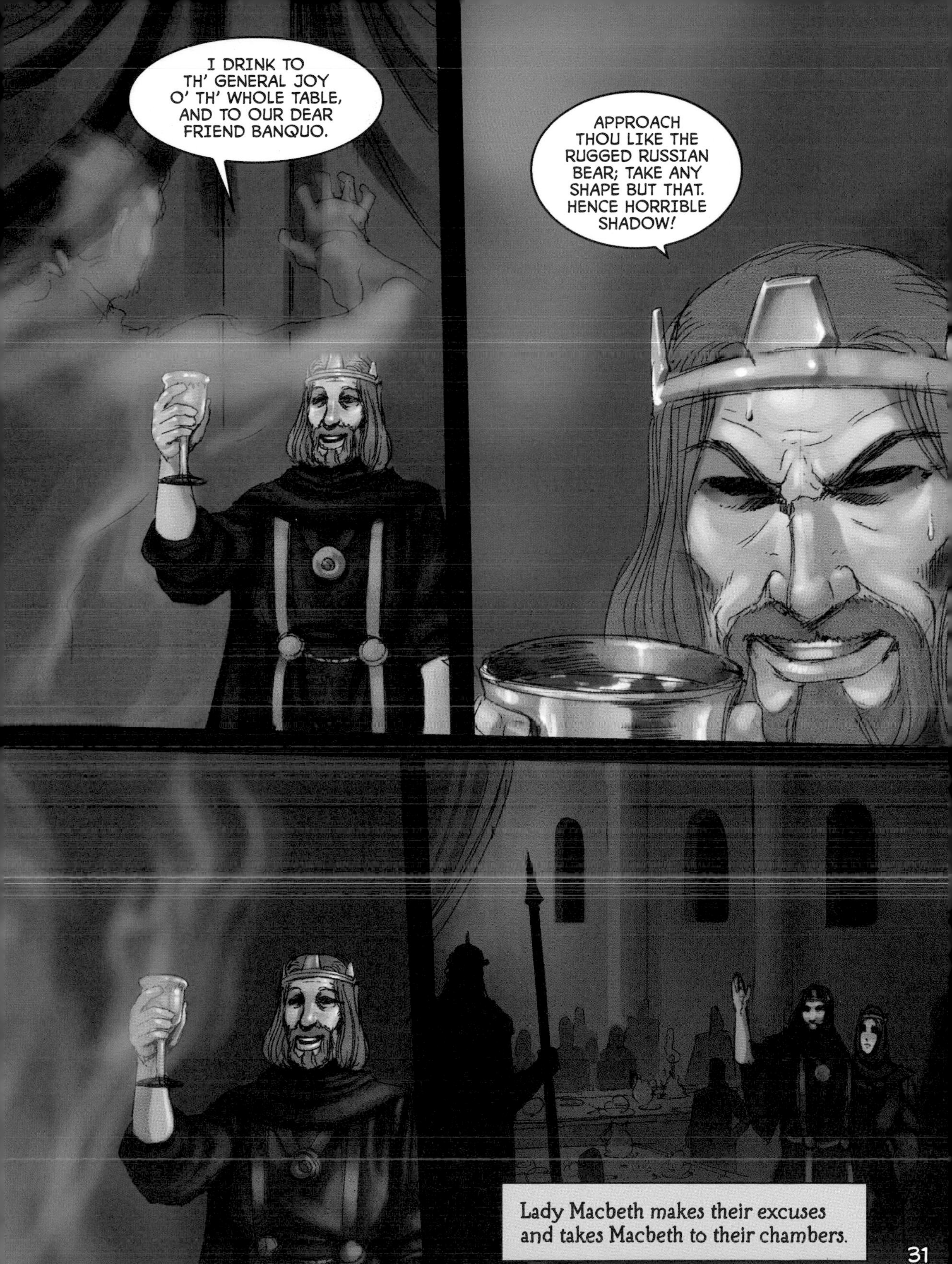
I DRINK TO TH' GENERAL JOY O' TH' WHOLE TABLE, AND TO OUR DEAR FRIEND BANQUO.
APPROACH THOU LIKE THE RUGGED RUSSIAN BEAR; TAKE ANY SHAPE BUT THAT. HENCE HORRIBLE SHADOW!
Lady Macbeth makes their excuses and takes Macbeth to their chambers.

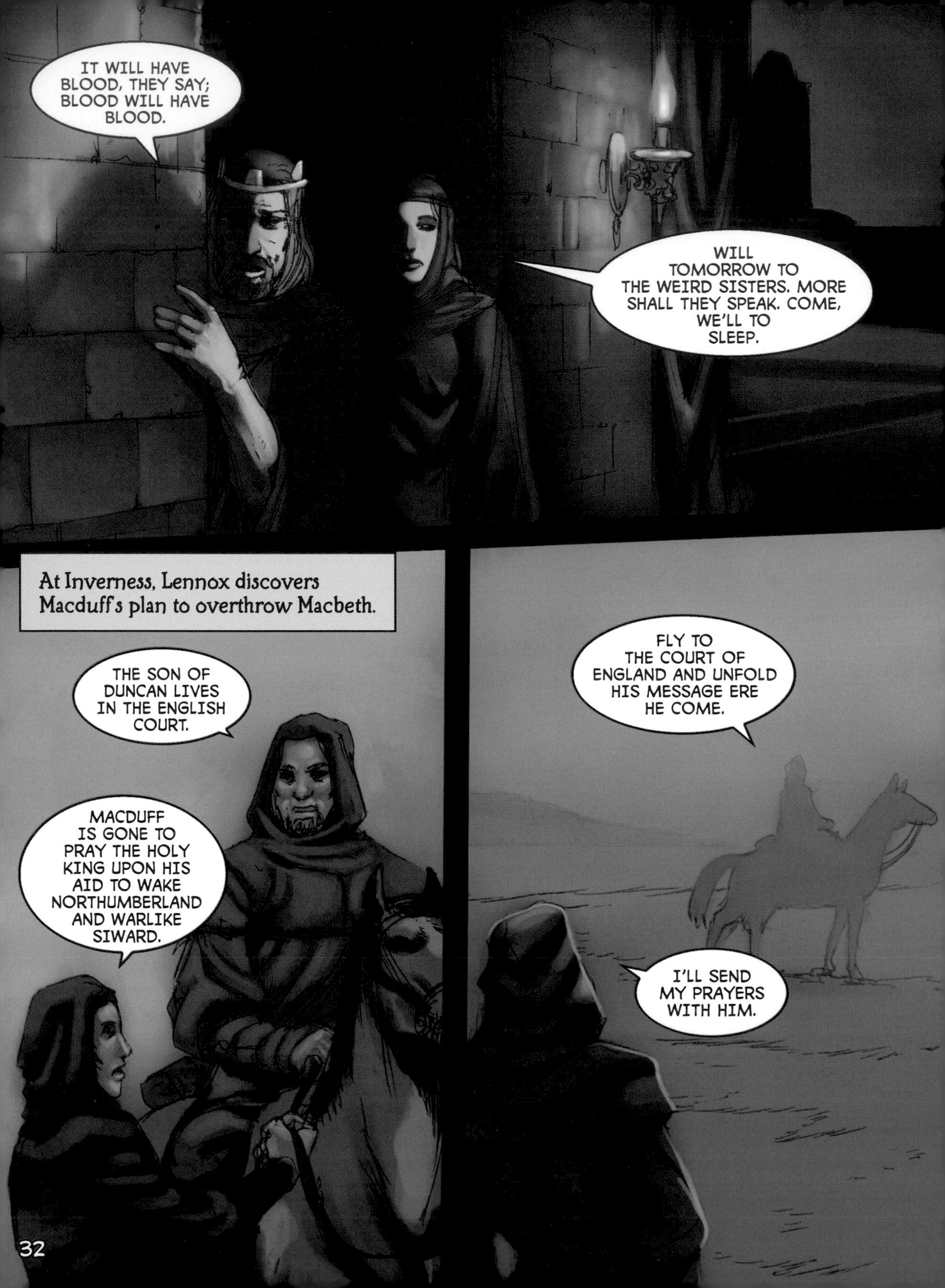
IT WILL HAVE BLOOD, THEY SAY; BLOOD WILL HAVE BLOOD.
WILL TOMORROW TO THE WEIRD SISTERS. MORE SHALL THEY SPEAK. COME, WE'LL TO SLEEP.
At Inverness, Lennox discovers Macduff's plan to overthrow Macbeth.
THE SON OF DUNCAN LIVES IN THE ENGLISH COURT.
MACDUFF IS GONE TO PRAY THE HOLY KING UPON HIS AID TO WAKE NORTHUMBERLAND AND WARLIKE SIWARD.
FLY TO THE COURT OF ENGLAND AND UNFOLD HIS MESSAGE ERE HE COME.
I'LL SEND MY PRAYERS WITH HIM.

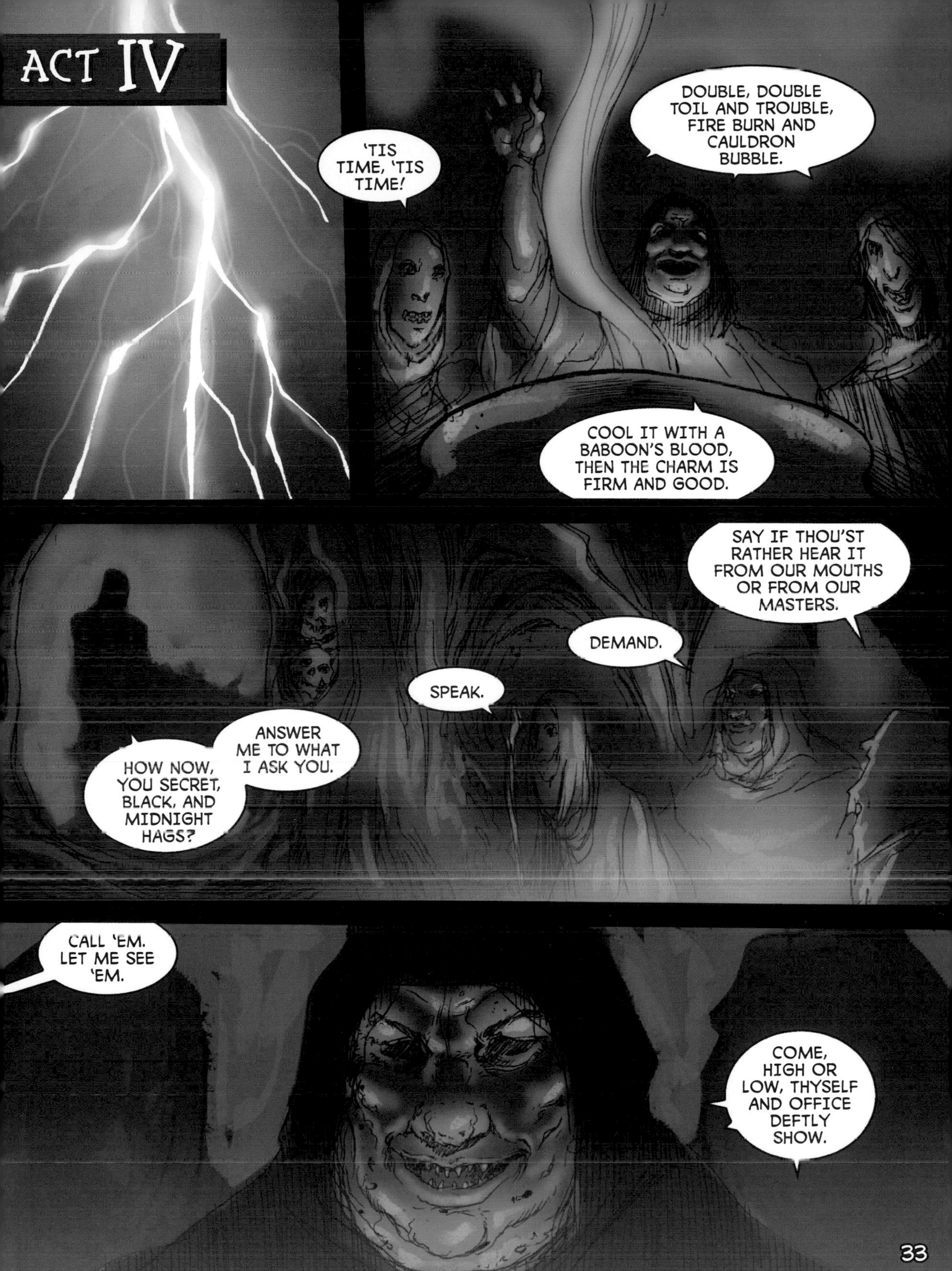
ACT IV
'TIS TIME, 'TIS TIME!
DOUBLE, DOUBLE TOIL AND TROUBLE, FIRE BURN AND CAULDRON BUBBLE.
COOL IT WITH A BABOON'S BLOOD, THEN THE CHARM IS FIRM AND GOOD.
HOW NOW, YOU SECRET, BLACK, AND MIDNIGHT HAGS?
ANSWER ME TO WHAT I ASK YOU.
SPEAK.
DEMAND.
SAY IF THOU'ST RATHER HEAR IT FROM OUR MOUTHS OR FROM OUR MASTERS.
CALL 'EM. LET ME SEE 'EM.
COME, HIGH OR LOW, THYSELF AND OFFICE DEFTLY SHOW.

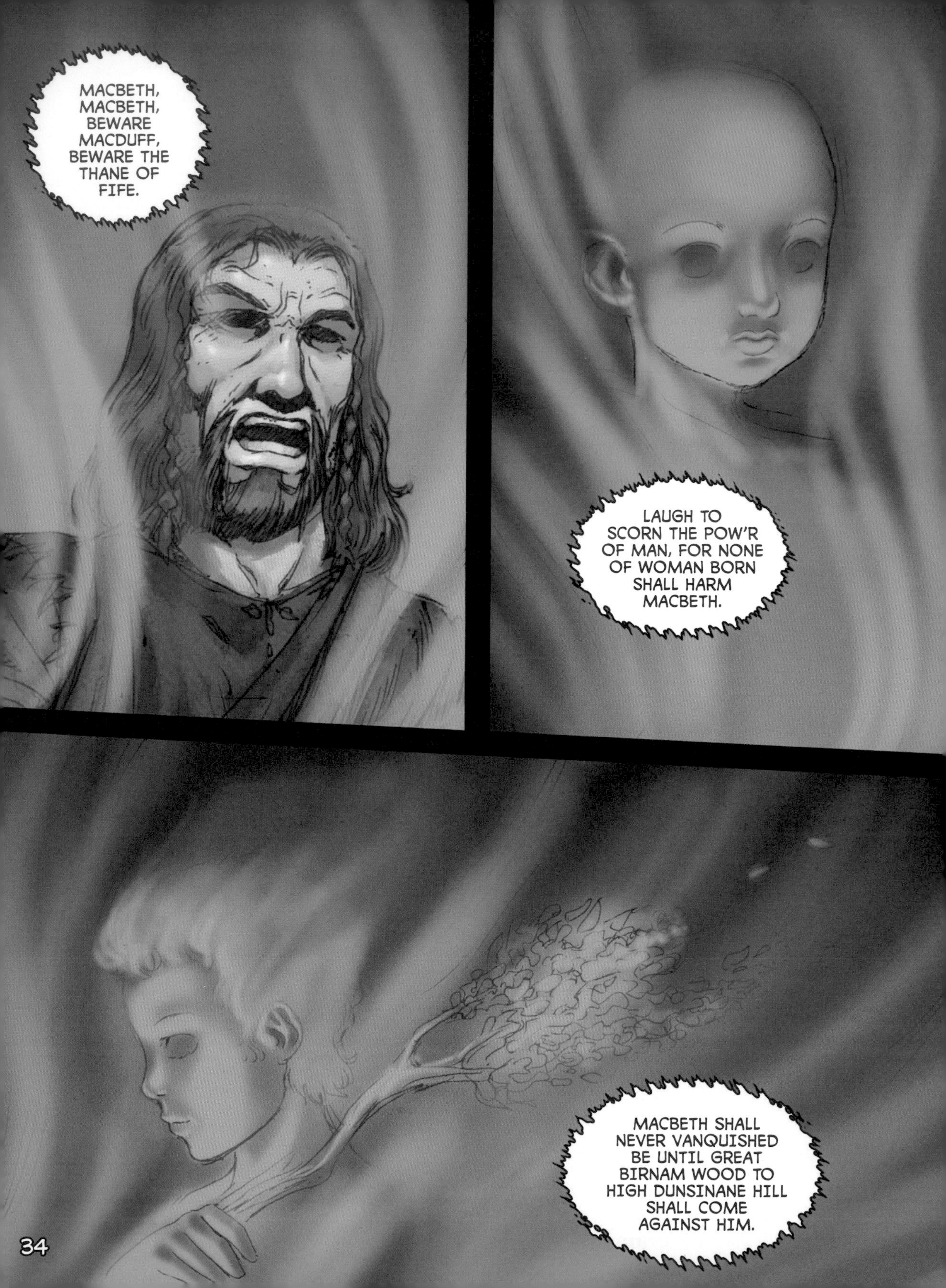
MACBETH, MACBETH, BEWARE MACDUFF, BEWARE THE THANE OF FIFE.
LAUGH TO SCORN THE POW'R OF MAN, FOR NONE OF WOMAN BORN SHALL HARM MACBETH.
MACBETH SHALL NEVER VANQUISHED BE UNTIL GREAT BIRNAM WOOD TO HIGH DUNSINANE HILL SHALL COME AGAINST HIM.

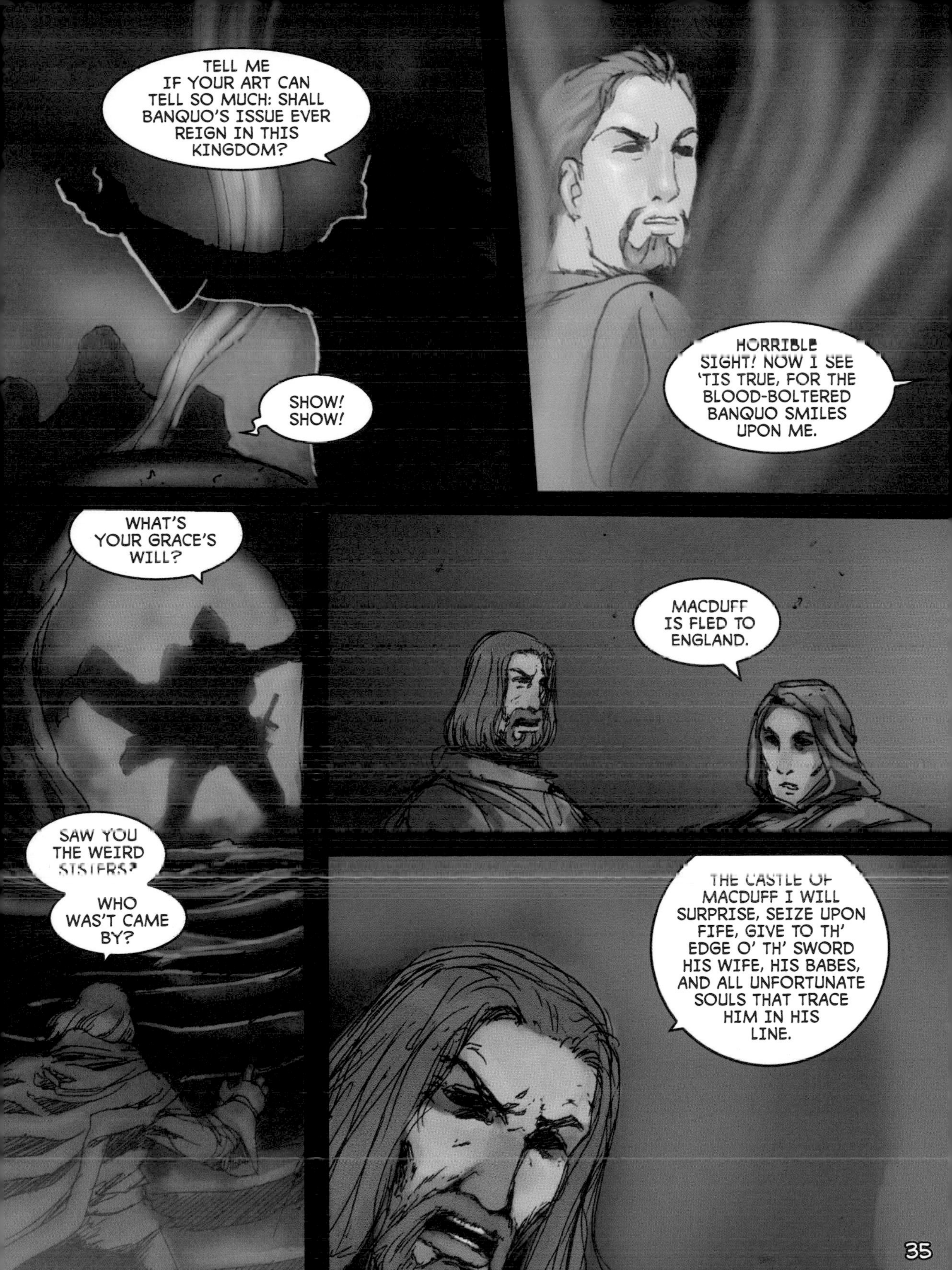
TELL ME IF YOUR ART CAN TELL SO MUCH: SHALL BANQUO'S ISSUE EVER REIGN IN THIS KINGDOM?
SHOW! SHOW!
HORRIBLE SIGHT! NOW I SEE 'TIS TRUE, FOR THE BLOOD-BOLTERED BANQUO SMILES UPON ME.
WHAT'S YOUR GRACE'S WILL?
SAW YOU THE WEIRD SISTERS?
WHO WAS'T CAME BY?
MACDUFF IS FLED TO ENGLAND.
THE CASTLE OF MACDUFF I WILL SURPRISE, SEIZE UPON FIFE, GIVE TO TH' EDGE O' TH' SWORD HIS WIFE, HIS BABES, AND ALL UNFORTUNATE SOULS THAT TRACE HIM IN HIS LINE.

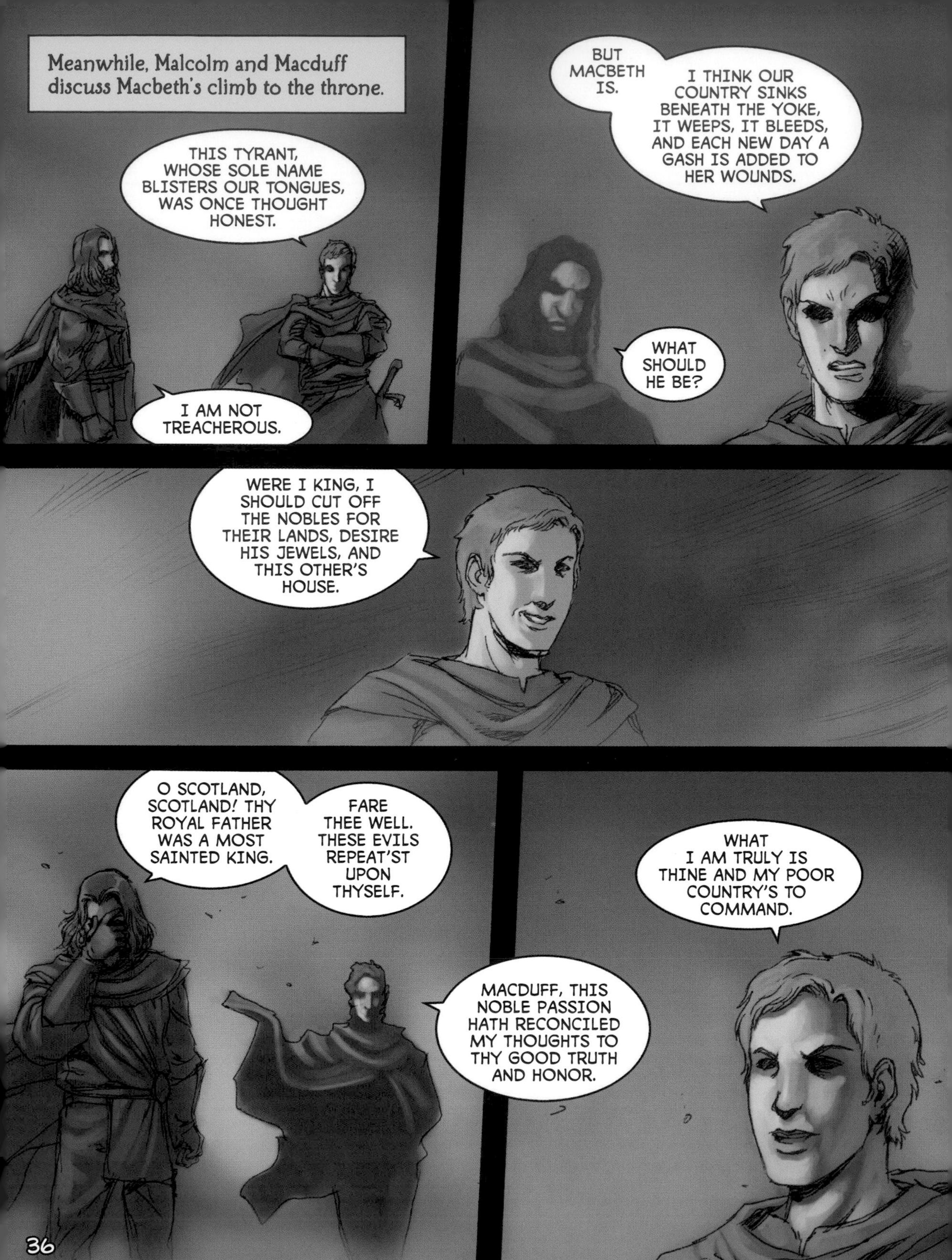

Meanwhile, Malcolm and Macduff discuss Macbeth's climb to the throne.
THIS TYRANT, WHOSE SOLE NAME BLISTERS OUR TONGUES, WAS ONCE THOUGHT HONEST.
I AM NOT TREACHEROUS.
BUT MACBETH IS.
I THINK OUR COUNTRY SINKS BENEATH THE YOKE, IT WEEPS, IT BLEEDS, AND EACH NEW DAY A GASH IS ADDED TO HER WOUNDS.
WHAT SHOULD HE BE?
WERE I KING, I SHOULD CUT OFF THE NOBLES FOR THEIR LANDS, DESIRE HIS JEWELS, AND THIS OTHER'S HOUSE.
O SCOTLAND, SCOTLAND! THY ROYAL FATHER WAS A MOST SAINTED KING.
FARE THEE WELL. THESE EVILS REPEAT'ST UPON THYSELF.
MACDUFF, THIS NOBLE PASSION HATH RECONCILED MY THOUGHTS TO THY GOOD TRUTH AND HONOR.
WHAT I AM TRULY IS THINE AND MY POOR COUNTRY'S TO COMMAND.

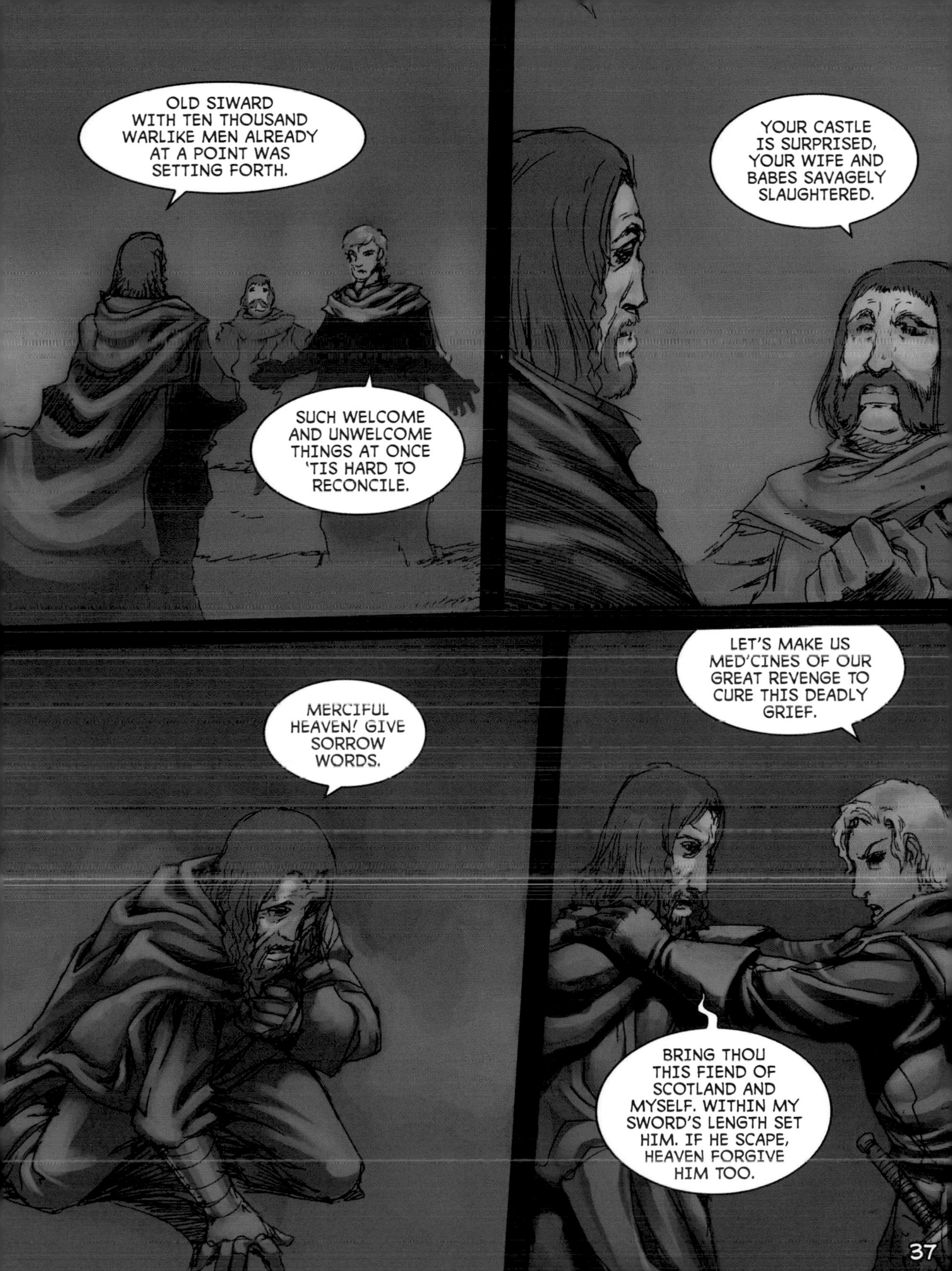
OLD SIWARD WITH TEN THOUSAND WARLIKE MEN ALREADY AT A POINT WAS SETTING FORTH.
SUCH WELCOME AND UNWELCOME THINGS AT ONCE 'TIS HARD TO RECONCILE.
YOUR CASTLE IS SURPRISED, YOUR WIFE AND BABES SAVAGELY SLAUGHTERED.
MERCIFUL HEAVEN! GIVE SORROW WORDS.
LET'S MAKE US MED'CINES OF OUR GREAT REVENGE TO CURE THIS DEADLY GRIEF.
BRING THOU THIS FIEND OF SCOTLAND AND MYSELF. WITHIN MY SWORD'S LENGTH SET HIM. IF HE SCAPE, HEAVEN FORGIVE HIM TOO.

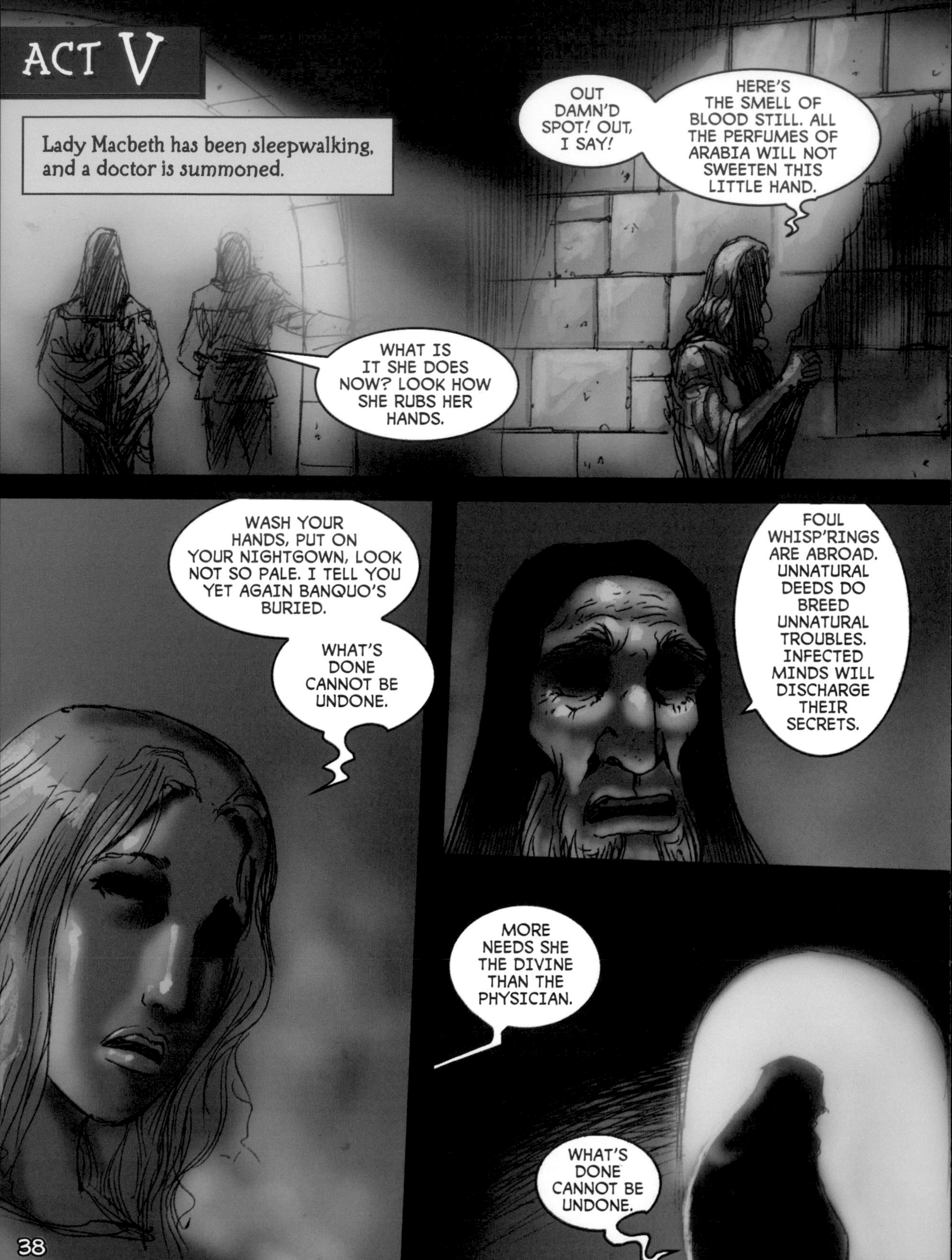
ACT V
Lady Macbeth has been sleepwalking, and a doctor is summoned.
OUT DAMN'D SPOT! OUT, I SAY!
HERE'S THE SMELL OF BLOOD STILL. ALL THE PERFUMES OF ARABIA WILL NOT SWEETEN THIS LITTLE HAND.
WHAT IS IT SHE DOES NOW? LOOK HOW SHE RUBS HER HANDS.
WASH YOUR HANDS, PUT ON YOUR NIGHTGOWN, LOOK NOT SO PALE. I TELL YOU YET AGAIN BANQUO'S BURIED.
WHAT'S DONE CANNOT BE UNDONE.
FOUL WHISP'RINGS ARE ABROAD. UNNATURAL DEEDS DO BREED UNNATURAL TROUBLES. INFECTED MINDS WILL DISCHARGE THEIR SECRETS.
MORE NEEDS SHE THE DIVINE THAN THE PHYSICIAN.
WHAT'S DONE CANNOT BE UNDONE.

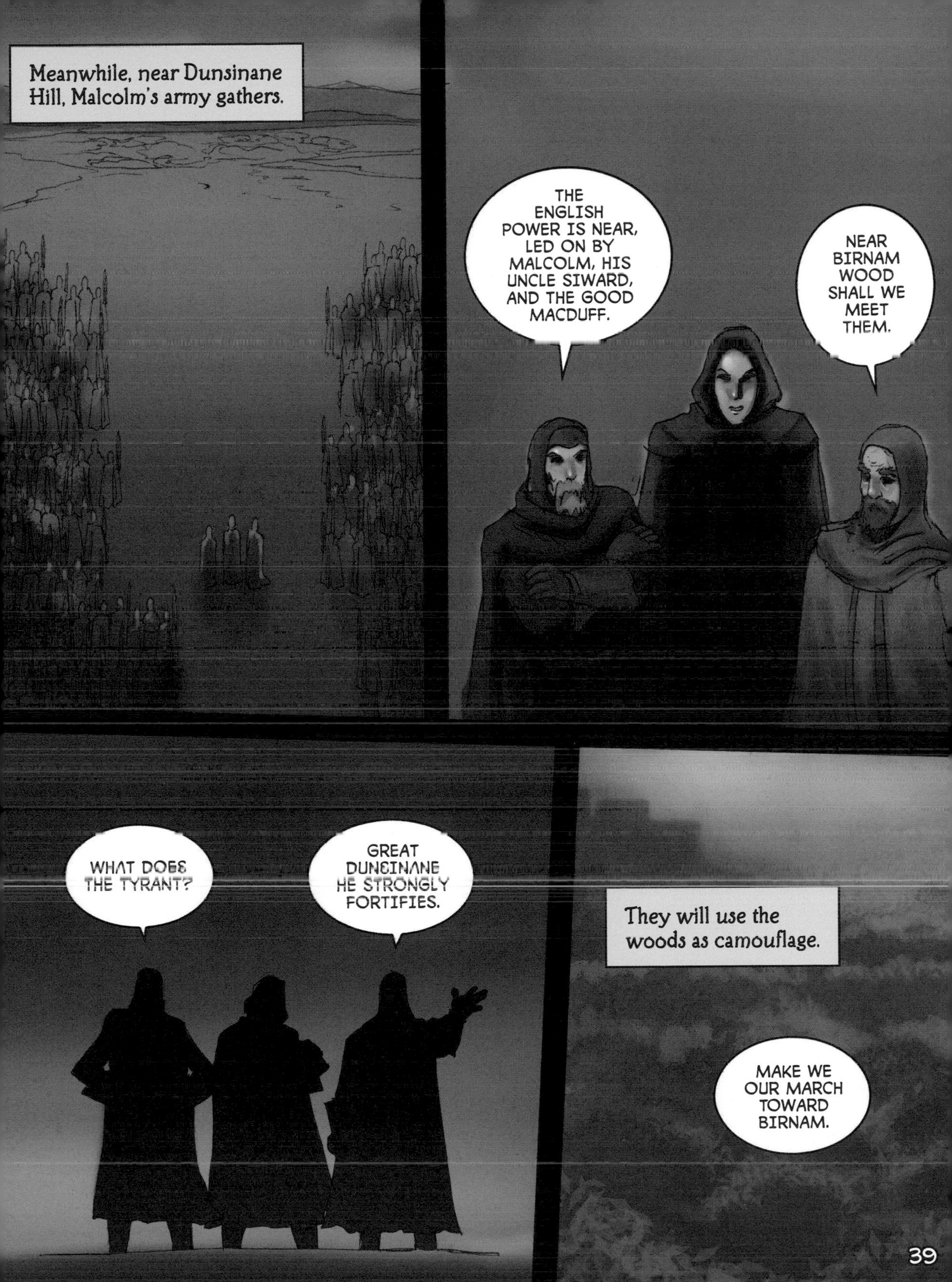

Meanwhile, near Dunsinane Hill, Malcolm's army gathers.
THE ENGLISH POWER IS NEAR, LED ON BY MALCOLM, HIS UNCLE SIWARD, AND THE GOOD MACDUFF.
NEAR BIRNAM WOOD SHALL WE MEET THEM.
WHAT DOES THE TYRANT?
GREAT DUNSINANE HE STRONGLY FORTIFIES.
They will use the woods as camouflage.
MAKE WE OUR MARCH TOWARD BIRNAM.

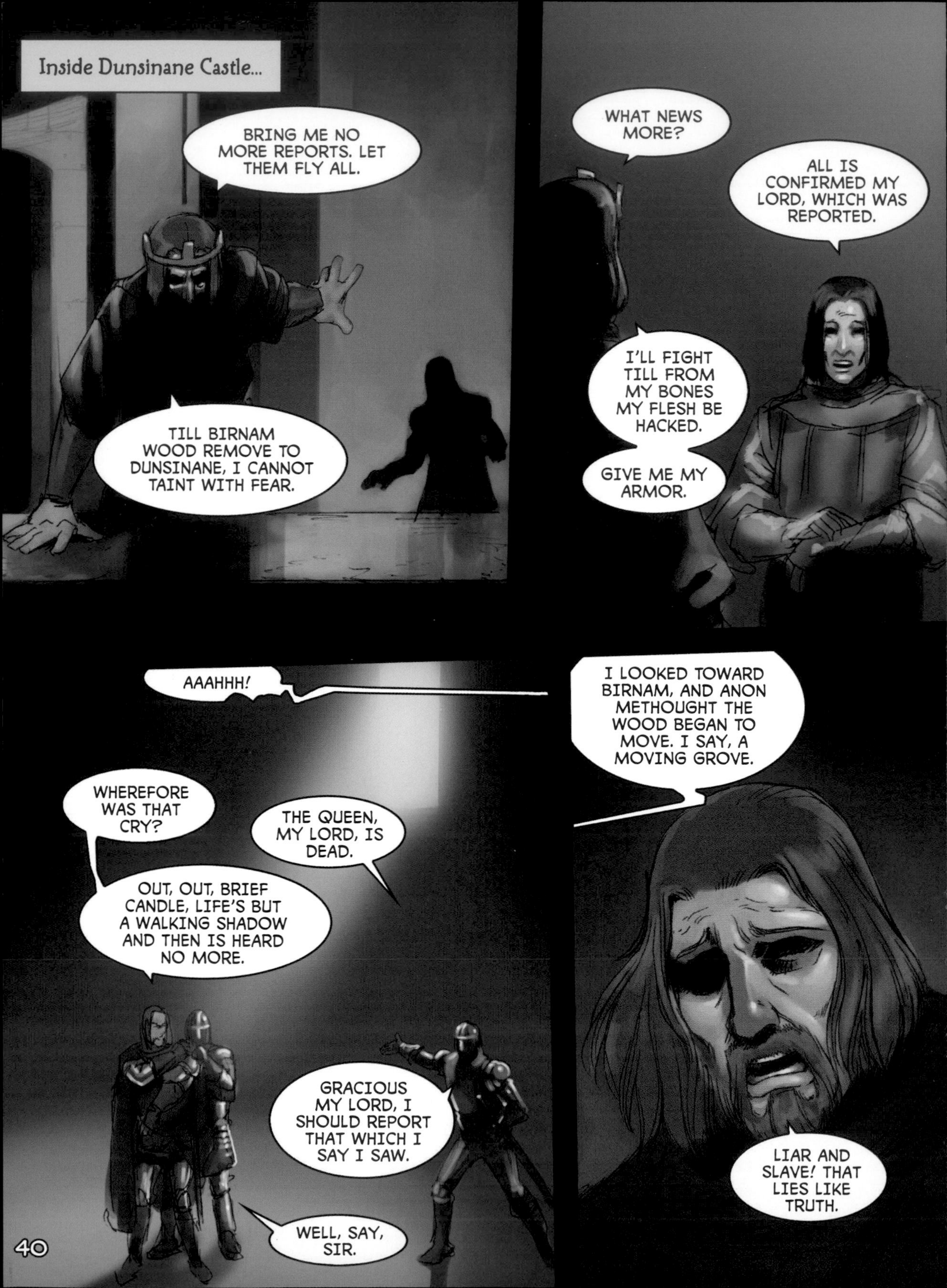

Inside Dunsinane Castle...
BRING ME NO MORE REPORTS. LET THEM FLY ALL.
TILL BIRNAM WOOD REMOVE TO DUNSINANE, I CANNOT TAINT WITH FEAR.
WHAT NEWS MORE?
ALL IS CONFIRMED MY LORD, WHICH WAS REPORTED.
I'LL FIGHT TILL FROM MY BONES MY FLESH BE HACKED.
GIVE ME MY ARMOR.
AAAHHH!
WHEREFORE WAS THAT CRY?
THE QUEEN, MY LORD, IS DEAD.
OUT, OUT, BRIEF CANDLE, LIFE'S BUT A WALKING SHADOW AND THEN IS HEARD NO MORE.
GRACIOUS MY LORD, I SHOULD REPORT THAT WHICH I SAY I SAW.
WELL, SAY, SIR.
I LOOKED TOWARD BIRNAM, AND ANON METHOUGHT THE WOOD BEGAN TO MOVE. I SAY, A MOVING GROVE.
LIAR AND SLAVE! THAT LIES LIKE TRUTH.

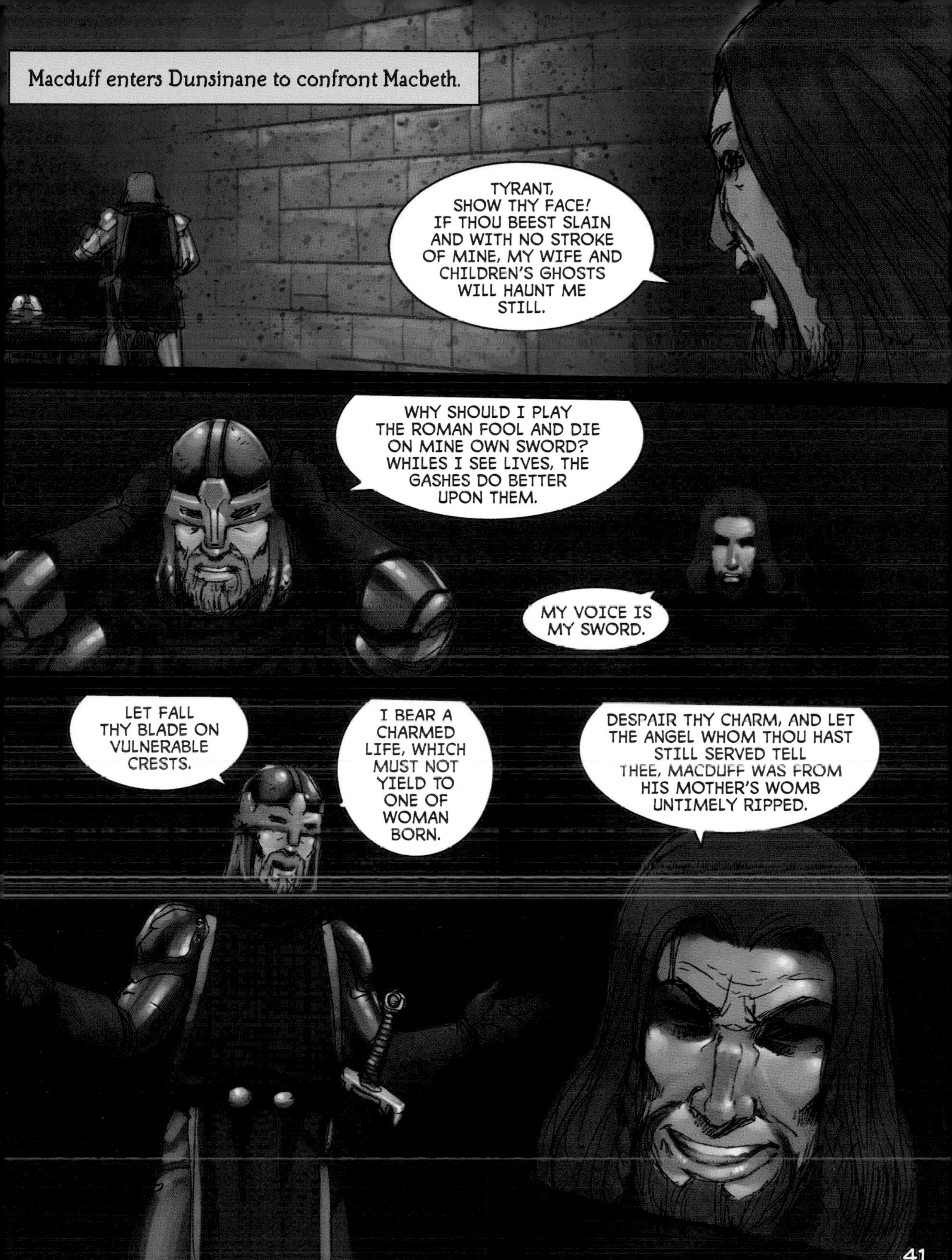
Macduff enters Dunsinane to confront Macbeth.
TYRANT, SHOW THY FACE! IF THOU BEEST SLAIN AND WITH NO STROKE OF MINE, MY WIFE AND CHILDREN'S GHOSTS WILL HAUNT ME STILL.
WHY SHOULD I PLAY THE ROMAN FOOL AND DIE ON MINE OWN SWORD? WHILES I SEE LIVES, THE GASHES DO BETTER UPON THEM.
MY VOICE IS MY SWORD.
LET FALL THY BLADE ON VULNERABLE CRESTS.
I BEAR A CHARMED LIFE, WHICH MUST NOT YIELD TO ONE OF WOMAN BORN.
DESPAIR THY CHARM, AND LET THE ANGEL WHOM THOU HAST STILL SERVED TELL THEE, MACDUFF WAS FROM HIS MOTHER'S WOMB UNTIMELY RIPPED.

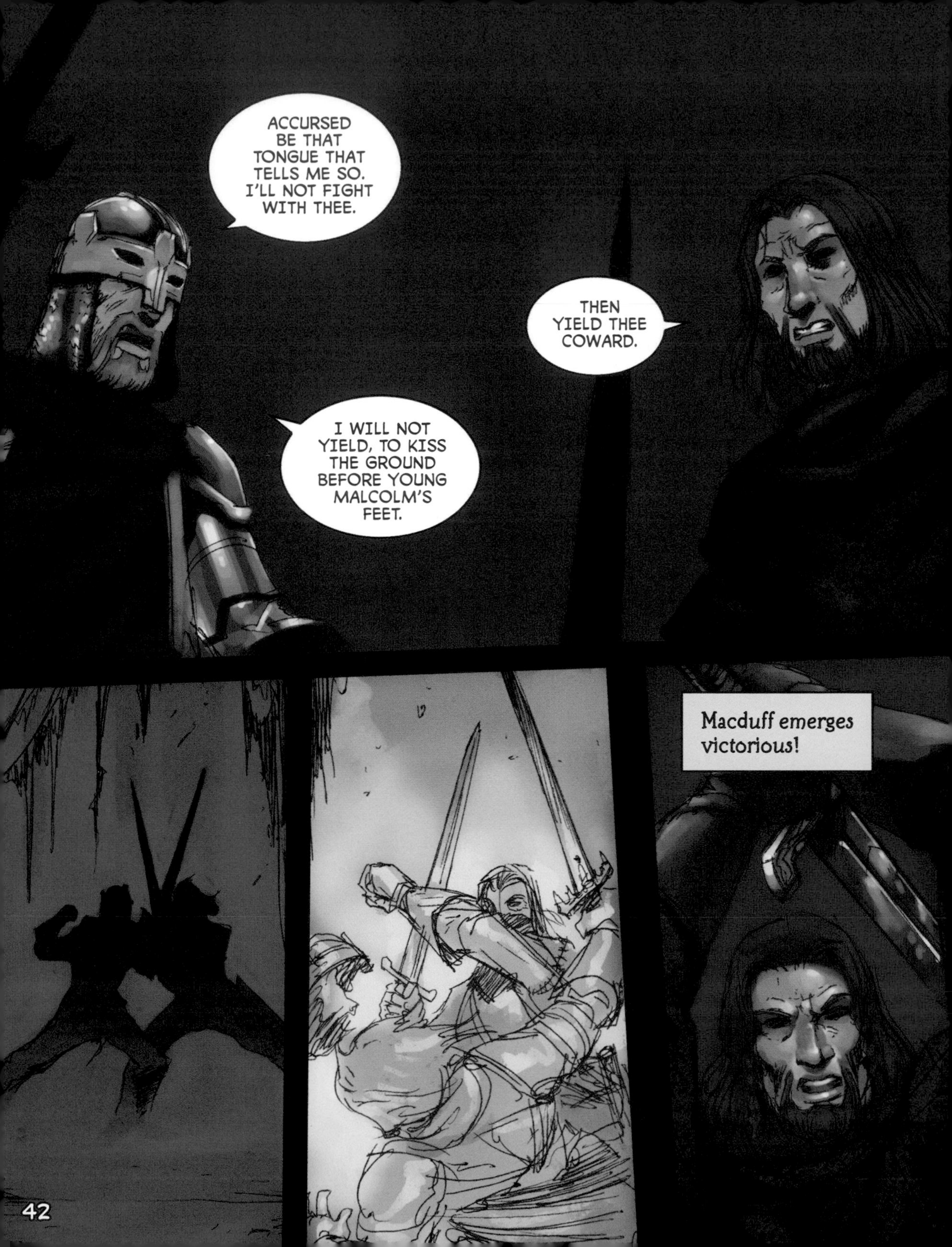
ACCURSED BE THAT TONGUE THAT TELLS ME SO. I'LL NOT FIGHT WITH THEE.
THEN YIELD THEE COWARD.
I WILL NOT YIELD, TO KISS THE GROUND BEFORE YOUNG MALCOLM'S FEET.
Macduff emerges victorious!

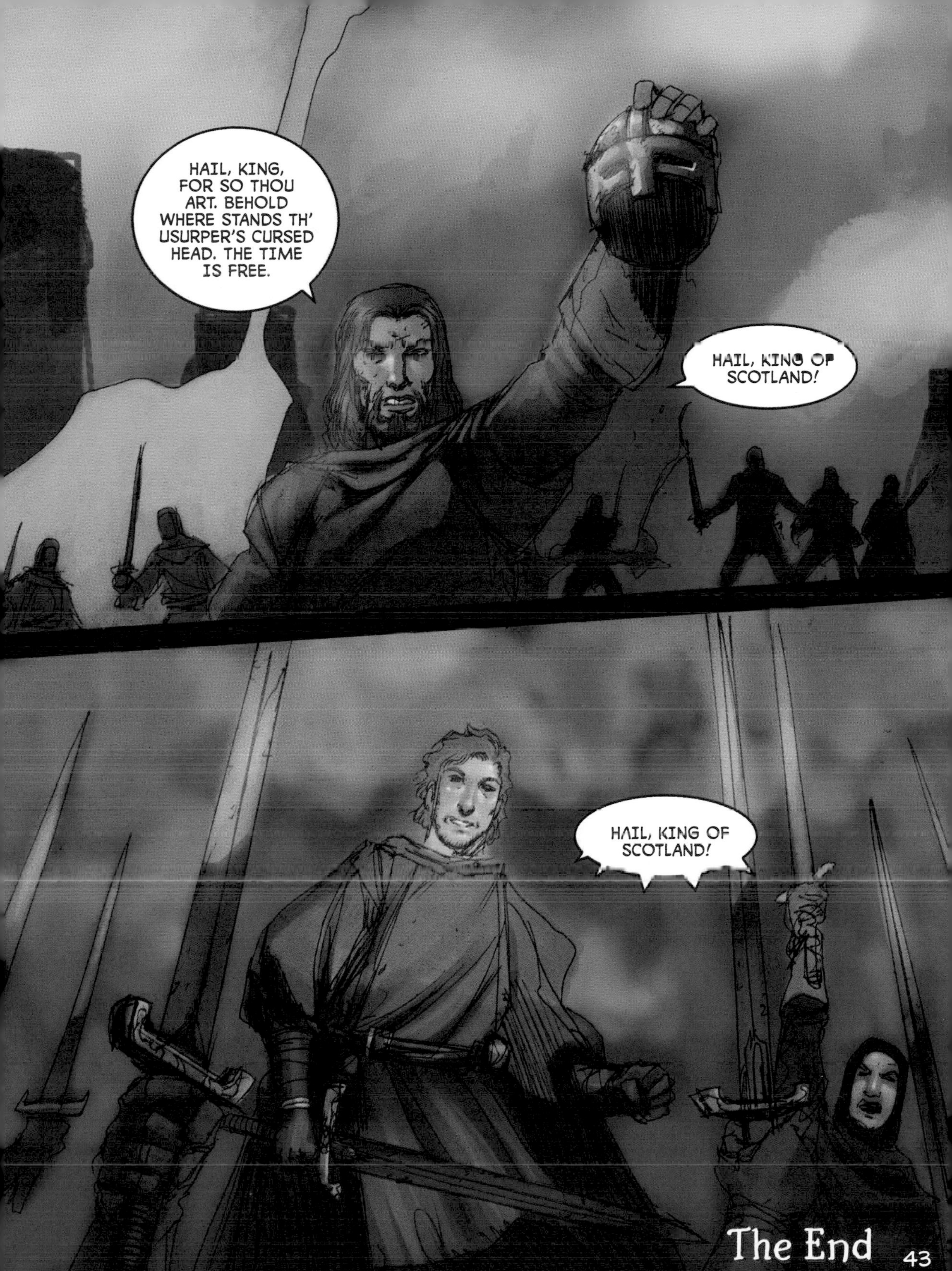
HAIL, KING, FOR SO THOU ART. BEHOLD WHERE STANDS TH' USURPER'S CURSED HEAD. THE TIME IS FREE.
HAIL, KING OF SCOTLAND!
HAIL, KING OF SCOTLAND!
The End

Discussion Questions

1. Do you think the three witches foretold events that would happen in Macbeth's life? Or do you think his decisions made it seem so?

2. The witches also make a prediction about Banquo's life. What are the differences in Macbeth's and Banquo's reactions to the prophesies? How do these reactions affect the course of events?

3. Consider the murders that are committed in the play. Do you think any are justified? Why or why not?

4. The witches proclaim that Banquo's descendants would include a line of kings. How does this prophecy affect events in the play?

5. When Macbeth was named Thane of Caldor it looked to be that the witches' prophecies foretold good for him. What events indicate they may have actually been warnings?

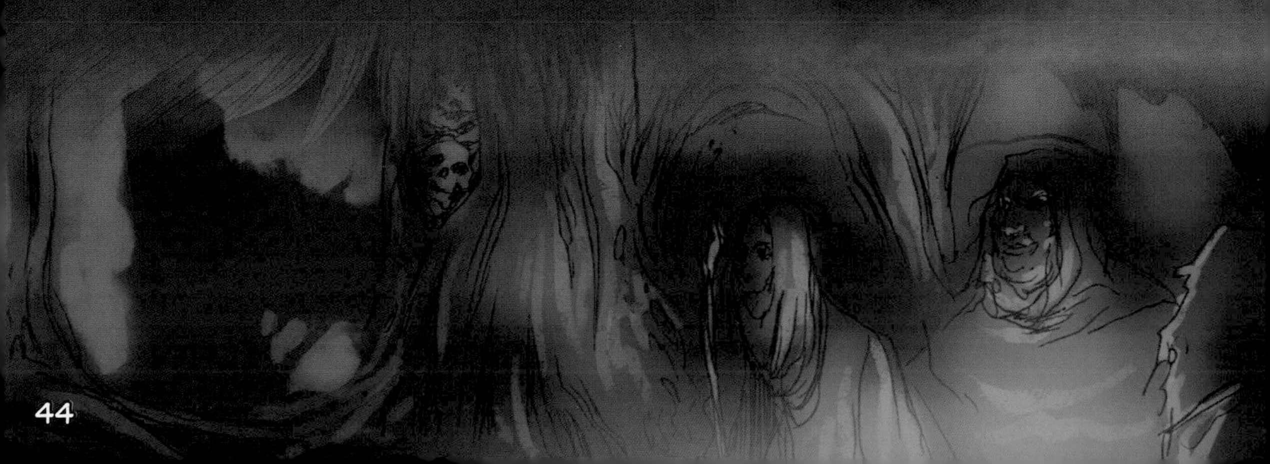

Fun Facts

- Macbeth was based on a real Scottish king, Mac Bethad mac Findlaich. Banquo was also based on a real Scot who was related to James I, the reigning king when Shakespeare wrote the play.

- Shakespeare wrote ten tragedy plays. Macbeth was the shortest.

- Some believe the play is cursed and will not refer to it by name. They call it "The Scottish Play."

- Macbeth is the only play in which Shakespeare uses the word rhinoceros. It is used in Act 3, Scene 4, when Macbeth is speaking to Banquo's ghost.

- The name Macbeth means "son of life" in Gaelic.

About Shakespeare

Records show William Shakespeare was baptized at Holy Trinity Church in Stratford-upon-Avon, England, on April 26, 1564. There were few birth records at the time, but Shakespeare's birthday is commonly recognized as April 23 of that year. His middle-class parents were John Shakespeare and Mary Arden. John was a tradesman who made gloves.

William most likely went to grammar school, but he did not go to university. He married Anne Hathaway in 1582, and they had three children: Susanna and twins Hamnet and Judith. Shakespeare was in London by 1592 working as an actor and playwright. He began to stand out for his writing. Later in his career, he partly owned the Globe Theater in London, and he was known throughout England.

To mark Shakespeare and his colleagues' success, King James I (reigned 1603–1625) named their theater company King's Men—a great honor. Shakespeare returned to Stratford in his retirement and died April 23, 1616. He was 52 years old.

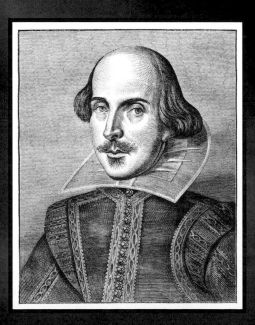

Famous Phrases

By the pricking of my thumbs, something wicked this way comes.

But screw your courage to the sticking place and we'll not fail.

Double, double, toil and trouble, fire burn, and cauldron bubble.

Out damn'd spot! Out, I say!

Why do you dress me in borrowed robes?

Glossary

accursed — being under a curse.

assault — a military attack involving direct contact.

furbished - renewed.

hurly-burly - the battle that is happening.

Neptune - the Roman god of the sea.

oracle - a priest or priestess through whom certain ancient gods, such as Apollo, answered the questions of their worshipers.

parley - to speak with another.

repentance - the act of feeling regret or sorrow for one's actions.

sacrilegious - dishonoring a sacred person, object, or place.

thane - a title for a Scottish noble.

wassail - bad behavior.

Additional Works by Shakespeare

Romeo and Juliet (1594–96)

A Midsummer Night's Dream (1595–96)

The Merchant of Venice (1596-97)

Much Ado About Nothing (1598–99)

Hamlet (1599–1601)

Twelfth Night (1600–02)

Othello (1603–04)

King Lear (1605–06)

Macbeth (1606–07)

The Tempest (1610-11)

- *Bold titles are available in this set of Shakespeare Illustrated Classics.*

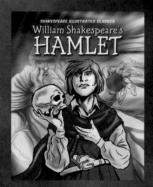

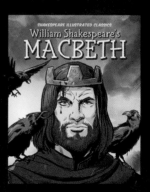

SHAKESPEARE ILLUSTRATED CLASSICS
William Shakespeare's
HAMLET

SHAKESPEARE ILLUSTRATED CLASSICS
William Shakespeare's
KING LEAR

SHAKESPEARE ILLUSTRATED CLASSICS
William Shakespeare's
MACBETH

SHAKESPEARE ILLUSTRATED CLASSICS
William Shakespeare's
A MIDSUMMER NIGHT'S DREAM

SHAKESPEARE ILLUSTRATED CLASSICS
William Shakespeare's
OTHELLO

SHAKESPEARE ILLUSTRATED CLASSICS
William Shakespeare's
ROMEO AND JULIET